Hidden in Plain Sight

A Journey of Ascension

John Flanagan
Meredith Harwood Flanagan

DIVINE LIGHT
PRESS

First published in Great Britain in 2017 by Divine Light Press

Copyright © 2017 by John Flanagan & Meredith Harwood Flanagan
Cover Design by madappledesigns

ISBN: 978-1542786065

First Edition

Acknowledgements

Laurie Hill – First draft read through.

Dara Lasky – Editing cover letters, synopsis, and first three chapters for submission.

Alyah Reid –Editing manuscript. Several incarnations.

Katherine Stroud – First draft read through, and advice.

Zlatco Kanda – Soul mandala on sleeve, and first cover.

Liz Gordon of Madappledesigns - The beautiful final cover.

Heartfelt thanks to Author and Mentor Michelle Gordon – For incarnating as a true earth angel. If anyone needs help editing and self-publishing. She's your girl!

To our teachers and guides.

All our love and gratitude for support and encouragement to family and friends in the UK and abroad. And to our Glastonbury community, spiritual seekers and pilgrims, twin flames and soul mates everywhere…
May you overcome adversity, in the throes of karma, and find true love in service.

In honour of the Divine Feminine in all Her glorious forms.

For Crea-Rose Flanagan

In loving memory of our ancestors and wayshowers –
Eilish and Martin, Anne, Morris, Roslyn, Eddie, Florence
(Chickie), Pop Pop, Stanley Shapiro, and Joel Goldsmith.

We hold these truths to be self-evident, that all men are
created equal, that they are endowed by their Creator with
certain unalienable Rights, that among these are Life, Liberty
and the pursuit of Happiness.

The Declaration of Independence July 4th, 1776

The red man will become white, and the white man red.

Hopi Prophecy

PROLOGUE

SWAMI ANANDA DAS
Ashram - Kerala, India
Present Day

Refreshed after only a few hours rest, Ananda savoured the precious silent moments while the ashram residents slept. Sitting at the edge of his cot, he was suspended in a depth of stillness that could only be experienced at the dawn of a new day. He watched the sun's rays cut through the fading darkness on the horizon, creating a golden crown. Droplets of water clung to the soft, dark whiskers of his beard after he cupped a handful of water to his face from the old basin on the floor by his side. He deftly twisted his long, wavy, ink-black hair around itself into a topknot.

He stood, and with his feet firmly planted on the floor, he patted down his naked body from head to toe and back again, rousing every cell, in preparation for a sequence of yoga asanas. The sun salutation had heralded the start of each day for Ananda ever since he was a child. His age now showed only through the greying strands around his temples, and the deep wisdom of experience in his eyes. He was lithe and strong, physically, mentally and spiritually.

As always, a small breakfast of idli and fruit had been left at his door. As always, Ananda wasn't yet hungry. He dressed, put the food and his belongings into a muslin cloth, and began his daily walk from the ashram to his private meditation hut, nestled within a wildlife sanctuary in Kerala, in the south of India.

A warm, spice-scented breeze flooded his senses as he pushed through dense, low-hanging brush, making his way toward the well-worn grassy footpath ahead. Myna birds chirped and whistled over the howling of grey Langur monkeys in the distance. Ananda was never lonely, even in his solitude. In fact, he had always felt more alone in a room filled with people than he ever did on his own, with only the sounds of nature for company.

With each and every step, as the soles of his feet met the earth below, Ananda gave thanks. He knew that it was the journey, and not the destination, that was truly sacred.

He arrived at his hut, hidden in the forested hills of the Western Ghats. Before shutting the weathered screen-door behind him, he took a moment to appreciate the expanse of eucalyptus, cinchona and acacia trees blanketing the misty evergreen forest. Soon, the world would wake and place its demands. But right now was his time to retreat, to take refuge in the sanctuary of his inner being.

Once settled inside the small wooden hut, Ananda removed his prayer shawl from the tattered sack, wrapped it around his shoulders, and knelt before an old acacia wood altar. As he lit a candle and an incense stick, he began to recite an ancient Sanskrit prayer. He then twisted into a cross-legged position, while chanting the sacred Gayathiri Mantra. With focused attention on his third eye, and breathing deeply and rhythmically, he entered into a transcendent state of total inner peace.

As his stillness deepened, the doors of perception opened and a faint voice pierced the silence. "I seemed to have loved you in numberless forms," it whispered. Ananda recognized these words instantly as the first line of the epic poem, "Unending Love" by Rabindrath Tagore, his mother's favourite poet. The words of Tagore's poem had imprinted themselves on Ananda's soul long ago, along with the memories of a cherished time with his beloved first teacher, the woman who had given him life. Still deep in meditation, Ananda recalled a time in his youth, sitting by the lake's edge with his mother. She had recited her treasured poems and stories from the Mahabharata while they waited for elephants to arrive for their evening drink at the shore. His heart softened as her essence filled his being and Tagore's poem continued to filter through his consciousness.

I seem to have loved you in numberless forms,
numberless times...
In life after life, in age after age, forever. My spellbound
heart has made and remade the necklace of songs,
That you take as a gift, wear round your neck in your
many forms,
In life after life, in age after age, forever.
Whenever I hear old chronicles of love, its age-old pain.
Its ancient tale of being apart or together.
As I stare on and on into the past, in the end you emerge,
Clad in the light of a pole-star piercing the darkness of
time:
You become an image of what is remembered forever.
You and I have floated here on the stream that brings
from the fount.
At the heart of time, love of one for another.
We have played alongside millions of lovers, shared in
the same
Shy sweetness of meeting, the same distressful tears of
farewell-
Old love but in shapes that renew and renew forever.
Today it is heaped at your feet, it has found its end in
you.
The love of all man's days both past and forever:
Universal joy, universal sorrow, universal life.
The memories of all loves merging with this one love of
ours –
And the songs of every poet past and forever.

Within moments, it was as if the poem's words were a key unlocking a door. While Ananda's body remained still as a statue in his hut, his soul was set free from its bodily cloak. His etheric body, unbound by the limits of time and space, began to travel at lightning speed across distant lands and oceans, as if he were being pulled magnetically towards an unknown destination. He had no choice but to surrender and let go. After some time, he felt himself gently slowing, until he remained, floating weightlessly, in one spot. His attention was drawn downwards towards a misty light, its origin was dimmed by a layer of dense, low-hanging clouds. Then, as if the Gods had exhaled, the fog was pushed along, and the unmistakable, outstretched arm of the Statue of Liberty's brightly illumined torch glowed, surrounding him with divine light.

He was relieved to hear the familiar, gently commanding tone of his primary spirit guide, a voice he'd grown to trust beyond question, a balm to his soul.

"The time is close. When the monsoon ends, you will receive your final initiation here. Preparations are being made."

Final initiation? Ananda wondered if he was being prepared to transcend the physical body once and for all. There had been a number of previous initiations, each of which played their part in educating his soul on its journey towards enlightenment. He had already undergone several earthly and spiritual tests following his life-changing accident, but the final initiation? The words lingered, reverberating like an echo.

Each previous initiation had been in preparation for this final imminent one: surrendering the human mind in its entirety to the divine mind's effortless grace. The human mind, with all its concepts, opinions, judgments and limitations, would ultimately submit in full and total trust. Once mastered, Ananda would then teach humanity, channelling divine instruction straight from the fountain of all knowledge and bliss, straight from The Source.

Ananda's awareness slowly returned to his light body, still hovering over New York Harbour. In that moment, his connection to earth felt tenuous, and many unanswered questions remained. He reached out and was comforted to feel that the lifeline that anchored his soul to his body was still intact. Then, in what could only be described as an experience akin to being sentient while still inside the mother's womb, Ananda felt as if the heartbeat of the universe itself was feeding him through a golden umbilical cord. He breathed in deeply and asked simply, "Why?"

A soft, yet powerful feminine presence emerged, cocooning him in pure, unending love. She whispered, "*Liberty Enlightening the World.*" The words trailed off into the ether as her extraordinary presence withdrew.

Suddenly, without warning, he was pulled back into his physical body. His eyes opened to see the comforting surroundings of his humble hut. The candle flickered. Ananda had only one thought – it is now time to go to America. He touched his forehead to the ground, acknowledging his surrender to the divine, and slowly rose to make his way back to the ashram to prepare for his journey.

CHAPTER 1

RICHARD DUNNE
Ananda's Ashram – Kerala, India
Four years earlier

On the top floor of a concrete tower block outside room eighty-seven, Richard removed his sandals and placed them next to an enormous pair of flip-flops. He stuffed his sunglasses in his pack and glanced up at the door, finding himself indifferent to the array of old, peeling stickers that covered it. The Om, the colourful Ganesh, and the ubiquitous Namaste, had all become symbols of his fruitless search for enlightenment. Richard had been in India for a while now and was exhausted, physically and spiritually, and yet, upon arriving at another ashram, he was surprisingly still a little hopeful.

A tall, wiry man with blond hair and glasses answered the door, seizing Richard's hand in a vigorous handshake. "Klaus. Klaus from Germany," said the affable stranger in a deep, heavily accented voice. "Welcome."

Richard was slightly taken aback by the enthusiastic greeting, but responded in kind. "I'm Richard. Richard from California."

"Nice to see you, Richard. My last roommate just left. Sorry about the mess."

Mess? After a cursory scan of the room's spartan, almost cell-like appearance, with its concrete floors and walls,

Richard wondered if perhaps Klaus was referring to the neatly folded pile of washing on the bed.

"To stop people jumping?" Richard asked, pointing to the iron bars on the window.

"You will get taken to the edge here, my friend, but only just!" Klaus replied with a chuckle, before noticing Richard contemplating the cramped corner where the small toilet and narrow shower stall were housed.

"The plumbing isn't always great," Klaus said, somewhat awkwardly. "Especially during the monsoons."

Richard tested the rusty tap on the sink, which was also crammed into the tiny corner, and gave a reassuring pat to a pair of Crocs tied to the outside of his pack.

"Good thinking," Klaus said, grinning as he gestured in the direction of Richard's bed. "Now make yourself at home."

Richard let out a huge sigh of relief as his backpack dropped off his shoulders and onto the floor with a thud.

"Believe me, Klaus," he said, heaving his pack onto the bed. "This is luxurious compared to some of the places I've been."

Klaus plunked himself down on the floor in the middle of the room, and watched Richard unpack.

"So what's the routine here?" Richard asked. "When can I see Ananda?"

"He gives a talk twice a week. One of the meetings is more of a question and answer session, but there are daily meditations, oh, and bhajans. You know, devotional singing, chanting, that sort of thing."

After taking inventory of the items given to him at check-in, which included a wash bucket and jug, a thin sheet, a pillowcase, and a flat musty pillow, Richard felt his energy returning.

"Some people get private meetings," Klaus continued. I've requested one every day, but haven't had one. An elderly woman from the UK gets one every day. One of his talks is starting soon, if you're up for it."

Richard dumped the nearly empty pack onto his bed and nodded. "Sure, why not?"

"I'm off to help out at the recycling centre, but let's head out together," Klaus said, appearing pleasantly surprised by Richard's burst of energy.

From a heavily embroidered drawstring pack, Klaus pulled out what looked like an old crumpled flyer. "Take this," he said, trying in vain to smooth the creases out of the battered piece of paper before handing it to Richard. "It's a map of the ashram. This place can get confusing."

"Thanks, Klaus," Richard said, chuckling at the condition of the map. "How long before you finish your gig?"

"I've got seva at the juice bar after I'm done recycling. Busy day for me."

"Seva?"

"Yes. 'Selfless service'. It's how the ashram is maintained. Everyone here, visitors included, offer their time to maintain the community. You should have been given that information when you arrived. There's loads of choices. Something for everyone. The more you give, believe me, the more you receive."

*

Richard sat cross-legged in the crowded auditorium, eager for the talk to begin, but also feeling restless and slightly ill at ease. He'd become jaded after a series of uninspiring stints at a few ashrams in the north, and started to wonder if the whole idea of an ashram was just a way to take money from innocent spiritual seekers. Richard had seen through the tricks and the mind manipulation, and having found no true spiritual sustenance, he had sort of looked forward to his return to his old, secular life.

Yet here he was, at another so-called holy place, which

he had decided would be his last stop before heading back to San Francisco. There had been no real reason for choosing this particular ashram, other than the fact that it was the closest to the clinic where he'd just spent a few weeks undergoing *panchakarma*, an ancient *Ayurvedic* detoxification program. The practice encompassed a series of personalized treatments that eliminated toxic conditions from the mind and body. Richard had completed the detox. He figured it would be a good thing to do before returning home to the States.

It certainly wasn't the easiest thing he'd ever done. The purification process was intense. An extreme amount of purging was involved, from all orifices, brought on by the consumption of vast amounts of ghee and strange herbal concoctions that tasted like a winter-blend potpourri, cinnamon, clove, nutmeg, and a host of other pungent medicinal plants. There were the daily herbal massage treatments that pressed and squeezed every last toxin out of each muscle fibre. Even thinking about it made him feel uncomfortable. After stripping his body clean of all toxins, Richard was given tinctures, vitamins, and the right diet to maintain the correct balance of his dosha, vata-pita. Richard had been physically and mentally drained by the whole experience, but he'd lost a few pounds, his eyes were shiny and clear, and he really did feel more balanced.

Today, however, he was feeling unwell. He'd enjoyed his first proper meal since 'the cleanse' just this morning, and for only ten rupees, it tasted amazing. Rice and fish served on a banana leaf with vegetables in a mild lime and coconut sauce. It had seemed like a good idea at the time, but as he sat waiting for the program to begin, he regretted the meal. He was nauseous, his stomach rumbled, and he was starting to sweat. He'd made a mental note of where the toilets were when he arrived, but had no idea how he would find his sandals amongst the hundreds of others, if he needed to make a quick exit.

Wiping the sweat from his brow, Richard closed his eyes and tried to refocus his attention away from his grumbling stomach.

"Are you ok?" asked a petite, flame-haired girl next to him. "You look a wee bit pale."

"My first meal after a detox," Richard replied without opening his eyes. Even moving his mouth made his stomach turn. "Not feeling great, but hanging in there. Thanks for asking."

"Try this," she said.

Richard opened his eyes to see her handing him a bottle. "It'll do the trick."

"What is it?"

"Water, lime juice, sugar syrup, some salts. It'll help you rehydrate and balance your electrolytes. You have to tread really lightly after a detox."

"Tell me about it." He took a few heavenly sips and handed it back.

"Uh, no thanks. It's yours."

Richard smiled, slightly embarrassed.

"I'm Sinead, from Dublin," she said, extending her hand.

Richard turned his head to the side, stifling a burp before extending his hand. "Oh man," he said, covering his mouth. "Please, excuse me."

Sinead seemed somewhat amused by his condition, but also genuinely concerned.

"So you're from Dublin. Yeah, I caught the accent. I'm from California, Richard. I mean my name is Richard," he stammered, trying to pull himself together.

"Well, hello, Richard," Sinead replied, smiling warmly.

"I just arrived at the ashram this morning," Richard explained. "I've been travelling for a while. Travelling and-"

"Detoxing," Sinead interrupted, with a twinkle in her eye.

"And detoxing, yes," he replied, smiling at her.

"I've been doing quite a bit of wandering myself. India is

a bit intense. You either love it or hate it, it's just that sort of place, isn't it?"

"Sure is," he said, with his hand on his stomach. "And I'm on the fence at the moment."

"I love it. It feels like God's land," she said, taking a deep breath. "You can feel it in the air. It's such a colourful place. The mandalas, the flowers, the saris, the icing-coloured temples, and Holi! An entire festival dedicated to colour!"

"I must agree. It certainly is colourful."

"It doesn't seem to matter how poor people are," Sinead continued, almost wistfully. "They look happy. They've got something we don't."

"And that is?"

"Faith?" Sinead answered, shrugging her shoulders.

Richard watched as Sinead lost herself in thought. He was touched by the candour of her earnest response, but not quite ready to concede to the innocence and happiness of the population he'd been living amongst for the past few months.

"I've seen too much on my travels to romanticise the notion of faith. India also has a dark underbelly, as most places do."

"Indeed, but not so much here. Kerala is a communist state, for a start. Crime is low, they have the highest literacy rate..."

Listening to her speak, Richard felt drawn to her. She was a true Celtic beauty with her pale skin, curly red hair and delicate features. He liked the way she smelled of patchouli and jasmine, and how she wore a shawl draped over her shoulders. With the string of wooden beads that graced her neck, she seemed a lot like the hippy girls on the Haight in San Francisco that his mother used to complain about, much to his chagrin. Perhaps most importantly, Sinead appeared to be a fellow seeker, a trait Richard found irresistible.

"*Ulysses*? That's a whopper of a book," Richard commented, breaking out of his reverie after noticing the book on the floor beside her.

"I know. One of my dad's favourites. He made me bring it with me, said I had to read it. I'm on my third try, and I have to say, I'm finally getting into it. Good thing, too. Only three more weeks in India before I head home."

"Well done for persisting. *Ulysses* was not a staple in the Dunne household."

"Dunne. Now there's an Irish name. I knew it! It's in the eyes."

"You're right. My father's family are from Wicklow, from way back," he paused, taking a deep breath. "I've never been, but according to my father, it's the Promised Land."

Richard looked away, covering his mouth again.

"Meal's still working its way through, eh?" Sinead commented, smiling. "If you need to make a run for it, go through that arch. It's closer than the toilets. You'll find a place to squat!"

"When in Rome," he said, forcing a smile.

"Indeed, Mr Dunne."

Richard drank some more lime water and his stomach settled a bit as he and Sinead shared stories about their travels through India. Richard talked about his time at the Krishnamurti Centre in California, and explained how a series of strange coincidences led him to India, a country he'd never before felt drawn to. Sinead shared anecdotes about her life as a secondary school teacher.

People continued to file into the already packed auditorium, and Richard looked around, shifting restlessly on his cushion, suddenly becoming aware of the increasing chatter.

"You're starting to go a bit pale again. How's the stomach?" Sinead asked.

"Stomach's fine, but my track record isn't so good with these places. Lots of charlatans out there."

"I know what you mean, but I think you'll find this will be different."

A hush came over the room, followed by the sound of

chanting. Monks in saffron-coloured robes entered the hall, followed by Ananda, a striking figure in white. They walked to the end of the room and stopped at the dais. One of the monks rang a bell several times. Ananda sat, while the others assembled at his feet. An oil lamp was lit, along with a stick of incense. Then the holy men began to pray.

Richard listened, taking it all in. Their prayers spoke to him, even though he didn't understand the words. The ritual reminded him of the Catholic mass from his upbringing, with the bells, the frankincense and the Latin hymns. Although he'd left the church years ago, Richard had always loved the ceremonies. It was only as he grew older that he questioned the doctrines and dogma. The concepts of original sin, purgatory and the threat of eternal damnation pushed him away from the church. He simply could not identify with the notion of a vengeful God.

Richard watched transfixed as the monks placed flower petals around Ananda's feet, then anointed them with sandal paste, and a milky substance before circling a flame around them, and then over his entire body.

"*Padapuja,*" Sinead whispered. "The worship of the guru's feet. Divine *shakti* is meant to flow from them."

This ritual reminded Richard of the biblical story of Mary anointing the feet of Jesus. He pondered the symbolism, and began to appreciate how interconnected everything was.

Richard noticed a strange high-pitched buzzing in his ear as he watched Ananda, who sat with his eyes closed.

The room was silent, yet it pulsated with energy.

Ananda opened his eyes to address the group. "Welcome everybody. Today's topic is the chakra system, and how each chakra plays its part in our journey to enlightenment." Ananda's voice was commanding, yet warm.

Richard looked around the room, and although he and Sinead were near the far end, he could have sworn Ananda was looking right at him.

"There are seven major chakras in the human body. The lower two are tied to karma and reincarnation. Balancing these lower frequencies plays a major part in our journey of ascension from the base to the crown, the alchemical journey to enlightenment. The laws of karma, the law that for every action there is a reaction, govern the first two chakras. When we vibrate at these lower levels, we are kept in the chains of karma. They are tied to the people and situations we meet over and over again, life after life. Their lessons are about me and mine – my position, my power, and my possessions. They are connected to the country you are born into, your family dramas, and your relationships. They hold your experiences of pain and pleasure, your desires, judgments and condemnations. Above all, they provide the opportunity for you to evolve. Each time we meet a person, or experience a situation that triggers us, we are given a new opportunity to react in a different way. When we finally chose to operate from love, respond with compassion, we will be given the grace to move upwards to the spiritual energies of the higher chakras, which contain our spiritual destiny."

Richard's mind was buzzing. He looked over to Sinead.

"Wow," he mouthed silently.

"Told you," she mouthed back.

"Aren't dramas, desires, and relationships a part of normal life?" Richard shocked himself by speaking out loud, interrupting Ananda. But he was oblivious to the glares from the audience.

Ananda moved closer.

"If that is the life you are comfortable in, you can keep reincarnating into similar relationship dramas and power struggles. At some point in your evolution, you will tire of them, and seek for deeper experiences. The soul longs to know itself. Only then will you let go of your attachment to the lower chakras and begin to open your spiritual centres. Everyone has a spiritual destiny. You have free will to follow it or remain where you are."

Richard's thoughts turned to his ex-wife, Mandy, and the years of unhappiness, one always trying to blame or change the other.

"How do you know if you're operating from your lower chakras?" Richard asked.

"Observe the need to defend yourself, or your point of view. That's ego. Be mindful that two people in any given situation will see things from their own perspective. Move out of defensiveness. External conflict is often about someone trying to convince the other of his or her rightness. The proof that an inner change has been made is when you attract situations that were giving you pain or causing inner conflict less and less, until eventually you don't attract them at all. Our outer life is a reflection of our inner life."

The words permeated Richard's mind. As he listened, he felt sleepy, as if he were falling into an altered state.

Ananda continued. "The third chakra is the bridge to the higher chakras; it is the bridge between matter and spirit. It is the bridge of selfless service, which leads to self-realisation. The more you are in service, the closer you are to spiritual wisdom."

Richard thought about Klaus working at the recycling centre. Again, there was a ringing in his ears, like he was being attuned with a tuning fork. He was starting to recognize it as a signal to be attentive.

"The higher chakras are doorways to other dimensions, where teachers and guides are waiting to work with us for the benefit of all. They bring you into alignment with your spiritual destiny, your divine purpose. Coming into contact with an individual who vibrates at the level of the higher chakras may give you an experience which lifts you out of the mundane, and gives you a glimpse of what it is to vibrate at the higher levels. This experience can speed up the process of completing karma by bringing your issues to the surface. This window into the higher worlds brings a momentary peace that goes beyond understanding, and plants a seed of desire."

Ananda walked around the room, allowing time for his words to sink in.

"The earth is also evolving through its own chakra system, which is interconnected with our own. You will be drawn to places which vibrate at the frequency you are currently working through in your physical body. These destinations will aid you in completing their lessons. It is not by chance that you are here in this land, which has birthed so many spiritual masters. All of you are being prepared to move up from the first two chakras, and step onto the bridge to begin the journey to self."

Richard saw Ananda's declaration as a call to arms, and he had a million more burning questions. In that precise moment, he knew that he was being called to something bigger than he could currently imagine.

Ananda turned his attention towards someone on the other side of the hall.

"A word of warning, however, if you artificially open the higher chakras, and you haven't properly worked your way through, as some have done through drugs like LSD, ayajuasca, or sometimes even through yogic practices, there is a danger of not being able to handle the frequency. Therefore, the advice is to accept where you are, and to kindle a deep desire to know your true self. Move slowly and gently ever upwards and ever inwards, letting go of the past. Cultivate unconditional love and patience with yourself first, and then others. You will be guided."

"Are there forces that try and stop us from fulfilling ourselves spiritually? Whenever I think I've changed, something seems to pull me backwards again," Sinead blurted out, keeping her eyes fixed on Ananda. She glanced over at Richard and smiled. His boldness seemed to have given her confidence.

"That's a very good question," Ananda replied. "Yes and no is the answer. The forces or external battles you are experiencing are not a power, but an externalisation of the human mind trying to keep us in the world that it has created, the world of illusion. The human mind has a fear of letting go, a fear of allowing the divine mind, which is incorporeal, to come into being. These forces that operate within the laws of the human mind feel like a power over and above us, but they are not. Love is the highest vibration. If you want to overcome something, send it love. If you want it to keep its power over you, simply react to it, and you will energise it. Each chakra goes through an initiation or surrender, so that the doorways of higher perception can open. We are tested a lot when we are getting ready to leave the first two chakras. Be patient."

"Thank you so much," Sinead replied.

An Australian girl in the back raised her hand. "Most of what you have shared resonates with me, but I've had a really abusive childhood. Are you saying the people who abused me also have a spiritual destiny?"

"This is difficult to understand, I know. But yes, they too, have a spiritual destiny. At some stage in this life or the next, they will seek higher understanding. They will realize the wrongs they did, and they will reach out for forgiveness, from you or from their creator. If they are humble and earnest, they will always get that forgiveness from the creator. The spiritual path is never easy. It requires warriorship. If you've had counselling, but still haven't managed to let go, the warrior aspect is needed for the final completion. The people you speak of need forgiveness. Forgiving them does not condone their actions, but by freeing them, you will free yourself from any chains of karma. The more you are able to do this, the closer you will get to moving on from those lower chakras."

"But they ruined my life," the young woman replied, fighting back tears.

"Or they have given you the blessing to be here in this room today. You can remain a victim, or become victorious by allowing a deeper understanding. This is a hard lesson. Get angry. Get counselling. But there comes a time when you must move into a higher understanding, and pave the way to forgiveness. The spiritual journey is challenging. Not many can follow its demands. Many seekers want the benefits, but not the struggles they must go through. They fight the process of letting go, the very process that initiates higher understanding. Initiation is always part of the gateway to higher consciousness. Being here is your opportunity to heal."

"I'm not sure if I am ready to walk this path, or if I even can," the woman said solemnly. "But I hear you, and I thank you."

"One step at a time," Ananda replied.

Richard realized in that moment that his soul had been crying out for recognition. And it felt as though his thirst was finally being quenched. All of his trials and tribulations, and years of darkness had led him to this place where he currently sat, in full surrender to Ananda and his teachings. He listened intently, absorbed every word and gesture, and cherished each glance. At one point, Ananda's form disappeared, and Richard found himself looking into empty space. *Am I losing my mind?*

"Yes," was the answer Richard received, and then Ananda's physical body reappeared.

"Be still," the voice said, coming from within. In that moment, Richard felt as if his aura was expanding to fill the room. His finite self was merging with his infinite self, his limitless self.

"What's happening?"

There was no answer.

Richard panicked, and his consciousness pulled back into his body.

"Finally," Ananda concluded. "It's important that those of you here in this room find real freedom. Do not set anybody up as your salvation, me included. Hear my words.

Find your truth. Take it back to your environment, your countries, and your homes. Let the ripples go out."

Ananda bowed to the audience, thanked everyone, and left the auditorium. His departure felt a bit abrupt to Richard, who felt astonished, bewildered, spent, yet excited. He'd had his first tangible spiritual experience, and he wanted more. The seed had been planted.

Richard and Sinead sat in silence and watched the crowd disperse. Both were at a loss for words, as if they feared that mundane conversation would intrude on what they'd just experienced. Eventually, they gathered up their belongings and said their goodbyes, and each headed back to their room.

*

Richard lay in bed huddled under his flimsy blanket, drenched in sweat. His body was burning up, yet he was shivering, gripped by a chill. He feared he might need a doctor, but was alone in the room and too weak to search for one. He eventually fell into a deep sleep. When he awoke hours later, despite relief from his earlier symptoms, he rushed to the toilet to vomit. He hung his head over the bowl, doing his best not touch its rim. He remained there for some time, head spinning, and stomach heaving. When the room finally remained still and his stomach was empty, Richard felt well again. Famished, he set off to find something light to coat his stomach, with the aid of Klaus' map.

Richard walked past the Ayurveda clinic, through the housing for the *bramacharis,* finally reaching his destination in a palm grove. It was obviously the place to be. It was teeming with people talking, reading, writing in their journals and eating. He heard the most wonderful chorus of devotional chanting in the distance, accompanied by spirited tambourines and intense, rhythmic drumming. A band of joyful, bouncing monks appeared from around a corner, followed by an elephant adorned with ornaments and colourful garlands. A crowd gathered as the group assembled in the centre of the courtyard.

Richard stood in awe of the massive, exquisitely decorated animal.

"His name is Razak. It means devotee."

The local man, dressed in a loincloth, made his way through the crowd carrying bunches of bananas piled high in a large bamboo basket.

"Ananda named him. He wandered into the auditorium one day – shuffled right up to him. Been here ever since," the local said, depositing a large bunch of bananas in Richard's hand before moving on.

Richard, having never been this close to such a large animal without the benefit of an indestructible fence between them, sidled up to the majestic creature with his offering. Carefully.

The elephant knew this game, and extended his trunk, stealing the bunch from Richard's hand. The local came back over and took the bananas from Razak, playfully admonishing the animal, plopped the bunch of bananas back into Richards hand, and wandered back into the crowd, stomping his feet in time to the drum.

Richard, not quite sure what to do at this point, offered them back to the animal. Razak looked into his eyes and straight into his heart, uncurled and stretched its trunk, and it proceeded to skilfully bite off and eat one banana at a time until they were gone.

"He's just an incredibly gorgeous beast, isn't he?"

Richard recognized the voice instantly.

"Sinead! We meet again!"

The two headed for the snack hut. They shared their thoughts about their experience with Ananda, over a mango lassie, and Richard told her about what happened afterward, back in his room.

"Already? Well you're on the fast track, aren't ya?"

"What do you mean?"

"Richard, remember what Ananda said in his talk? That when you are around someone like him, who is vibrating at a higher chakra level, everything gets sped up? You're burning up karma. You'll see how much you've changed once you leave and get back to your life in America."

"I imagine it was probably just my body still ridding itself of toxins after my detox," Richard said wryly. *Or perhaps it is?*

During their time at the ashram together, Sinead would become an indispensable source of counselling and companionship for Richard. She seemed to cross his path whenever he needed a question answered, or a friend to talk to. The week before she left for Varkala, they'd taken a couple of day excursions together to explore the surrounding landscape. Richard had grown incredibly fond of Sinead, but despite the fact that he found her attractive, he saw her in a sisterly way, rather than as a potential lover. She felt like family to him. *Or did she?*

"How much longer are you gonna stay for?" she asked before leaving.

"A couple of weeks, I think, and then I'm heading back home."

Five days before Richard was due to leave the ashram, he was blessed with a personal interview with Ananda.

The two men spent less than five minutes together in silent meditation. Shortly after, Richard had a strong feeling that he should remain at the ashram. He'd come to understand that his devotion to Ananda was absolute. He'd known this on some level since the first time he'd seen him, but he still experienced a feeling of apprehension over his decision to stay longer. Ananda had advised Richard to put his affairs in order, apply for an extended visa, and not to worry. He let Richard know that everything would fall into place, and that his blessing was with him.

It would be four years before Richard would set foot back in the country of his birth.

CHAPTER 2

ROSE COHEN
New York City
Mid-June, Present Day

Every day was the same… wishing the world would go away, wanting life to be different.

You have to get over the incident, darling, her mother's insistent voice droned in her head. *You have to move on from the incident, sweetheart.*

"Incident? Stop calling it an incident!" Rose screamed out loud, as if her mother were in the room. Her face flushed with anger as she went over the distressing event in her head. Sadie and Adam eating at *their* favourite restaurant – Del Vecchio's in Little Italy. Rose cringed at the thought of Sadie laughing flirtatiously at Adam's bad jokes.

Oh c'mon, Sade! You know they're awful!

Sadie and Adam in bed together. *Our bed!* That was the worst part. Betrayed by her husband and her best friend, in *her* home. No matter how much inner work she did to let go and cut the ties to the incident, she just couldn't move on.

Her bedroom door creaked open.

"Rose, darling, are you okay? I heard a scream." The overly concerned tone in her mother's voice was both comforting and completely irritating.

"I'm fine," Rose said, lowering her eyes from her mother's gaze. "Just a bad dream."

"Honey, it's almost one. Don't you think you should get dressed?"

Do I think I should get dressed? Really? I think it's perfectly normal for a forty-year-old woman to sleep the morning away in her childhood bedroom.

"I just can't, Mom. Not yet."

Her mother sat on the edge of the bed, and rested her hands heavily on Rose's thin shoulders. "It's time."

"I have nowhere to go," Rose said, pushing her away.

"I meant that it's time to address this. Come on."

"Mom, please leave me alone," she whined. "I'm not a teenager anymore."

Her mother stood up, sighed impatiently and walked out, shutting the door behind her.

Rose got out of bed and went over to the window. She perched on the window ledge and looked past the fire escape at the hustle and bustle of the street below. The building occupied a prime spot on Madison Avenue. Her family had owned the building and run their business there for two generations. *What do I do now? Where do I go from here?* Her heart skipped a beat and then another, and then it ran a marathon. *Am I having a heart attack or a stroke?* Her thoughts raced as fast as her heart, and it felt like her brain was pounding against the edges of her skull as though it were trying to escape.

Feeling anxious, Rose went back to her bed and lay down. She stared at the intricate pattern on the ceiling, something she had done throughout her childhood. It served as a meditation, a calming point of focus, which helped her make sense of things while she soul searched. She breathed slowly, in through her nose and out of her mouth, in a bid to quell her anxiety, just as Dr. Rifkin had taught her. As she calmed, she began to recall the dream that had awoken her. She had been trapped inside a lion's cage at the circus. The crowd were yelling at her to move slowly backwards towards the gate. But as the lion advanced, her legs wouldn't budge.

She had screamed at the top of her lungs, but no sound had come out.

Remembering her terrifying dream wasn't helping Rose calm her anxiety, so she closed her eyes and concentrated purely on her breathing. After a few moments, she drifted off to sleep and straight into another dream. She found herself in a rowboat, being tossed about in a raging sea, at the mercy of an angry ocean that threatened to capsize her. In the distance, she saw a lighthouse. Hope filled her heart, and in that moment, the ocean calmed and her boat and her soul became still.

Maybe it isn't too late for me, she thought upon waking. Looking around her room with new eyes, she felt grateful to be in supportive and safe surroundings.

"Rose, it's lunchtime!" Her mother's voice startled her out of her thoughts.

"I'll be down in a little while!" she shouted back, surprised that food actually sounded appealing.

Sliding out of bed, Rose went to stand in front of the full-length antique mirror. She winced at the sight of her wild hair, and white cotton nightgown hanging loosely over her small frame. *I look like an escapee from a psychiatric hospital.* Moving closer, she looked deeply into her own eyes, and for the first time in months, recognized a spark of her old self. For a split second, she thought she felt her grandmother's presence, and could almost smell Oil of Olay face cream and L'Air de Temps perfume.

She sat down in the rocking chair that had lulled two generations. It had been a fixture in her room since her grandmother's passing when Rose was in the fourth grade. She reminisced about the many sleepovers at Grandma's, who lived only a staircase away.

In her mind's eye, Rose recalled watching the gentle and measured mannerisms of her Grandma as she prepared for bed. Slipping off her stockings and unhinging her girdle to release silky, sagging skin from the shackles. Her nakedness was both shocking and awe-inspiring to Rose. She had loved every inch of the timeworn woman, with her wisps of grey hair and proud, frail beauty.

She thought of their endless games of 'house' and 'beauty parlour'. *She was so patient.* In the present moment, she wished she could crawl into bed with Grandma, nestle in her arms, safe and adored. *Unconditional love.* Looking upwards as if she could see through the ceiling and into her childhood, Rose was reminded that nothing remained inside the apartment above, aside from cherished memories, storage boxes, and store stock. Tears formed in her tired eyes and she cried, for her own sorrows, as well as the struggles and sorrows of her ancestors.

The smell of matzo brei wafted into her room from the kitchen down the hall, reminding Rose of how much she loved to watch her grandmother cook specialties that had been handed down through generations. Potato latkes, blintzes, knishes, borscht, brisket of beef – the list was endless. Rose recalled her grandmother flipping a potato pancake in sizzling oil, while declaring that the most important ingredient was love. "You're the tester, Rose. Make sure they are crispy enough."

Rose followed the smell down the hall towards the kitchen, passing through a gallery of family portraits lining the hallway. She took comfort, and felt guarded by the portraits of her ancestors looking out of their frames like ghosts. She paused at each one, retrieving their stories, while trying to make sense of her own.

The first picture was of Selda and Morris on their wedding day. *You were so pretty,* Rose thought, admiring the photograph. *You were a lucky man, Morris Cohen.* Soon after, they would leave everyone and everything they had ever known and loved. *She must have really trusted him to come all this way.*

Their wedding present had been a one-way transatlantic crossing and a permanent honeymoon in the United States.

As Jews from Russia, they had passed through the gateway of Ellis Island in the early 1900s, and crossed over the threshold into their new world as Americans. They carried only a few precious items, which had fit into their suitcase and an old steamer trunk.

Rose studied the photograph again, recognizing the prayer shawl around Morris' shoulders as the same one her father, Samuel, wore during the Sabbath prayers. It had belonged to her great-grandfather, and had been a treasured heirloom of the Cohen family for generations. It was called a *tallit*, and family lore was that it had a connection with the Kohenim, the first priests in the Temple of Jerusalem. Every Friday night, at exactly eighteen minutes before sundown, Selda had lit the candles, then circled her hands around the flames, held her palms in front of her eyes and said the Sabbath prayer, remembering all the family and friends they'd left behind.

"God bless them," she had said and then spat three times for good luck. This tradition died with her. Rose's father had never been particularly religious, and had later married outside of the faith, which had not gone down well.

Her grandparents' story was an American success story, etched in every fibre of the building. Morris and Selda's new life had begun in a tenement apartment on Manhattan's overcrowded lower East Side. But with Morris' drive and business acumen, the couple had soon saved up enough – by selling from a grocery cart – to rent a shop with a small apartment overhead. *Cohen's* was born. It was a homey place, the grocery and cafeteria had catered to new immigrants, mostly from Eastern Europe and Russia, and was for many, a second home where they found comfort reminiscing about their homeland and speaking their native languages as they integrated into their new lives. Cohen's had quickly gained a reputation on the docks of New York City as the place to go for a warm welcome. Morris and Selda were among the few who prospered at that time, and with determination, faith, and trust, they eventually purchased, then sold, the original site of Cohen's. By the time Samuel, Rose's dad, was a toddler, they had put a down payment on this very building in the Upper East Side on Madison Avenue.

The cured meats, smoked fish, pickled veggies and boiled sweets moved to a small space in the back of Cohen's new store, while imports from France took centre stage, catering to more modern tastes. Morris had a fondness for good champagne and wine, and spent much of his later years collecting the finest bottles from around the world – Chateaux's La Fite, Margot, Dom, and Veuve Clicot – which waited patiently for their time to shine, and shine they often did. The best of Cohen's wine cellar had graced weddings, bar mitzvahs, birthdays and a host of other special occasions.

With its elegant atmosphere and air of old-world charm, the newly named *Maison* became one of the top destinations for people visiting New York. Often frequented by the city's financial and cultural elite, Maison evolved into a high society hot spot. It had that special something. It was a cultural landmark of historical and social significance, that still managed to give one the feeling of visiting a very sophisticated old friend's living room.

Rose made her way down the hall, stopping at each frame, greeting each ancestor, ending up at the last photograph. It was of her great-grandfather. He stood proudly in front of a country house. It was one of the few pictures of her mother's side of the family that they had, and it was still in its original frame. *He looks like a noble and learned man with that book and cane,* she thought. *Is that a bible?* Curious to find out, Rose carefully took if off the wall, and peered at the picture more closely. Her great-grandfather's eyes penetrated hers.

"Turn it over," Rose heard in her mind. Frowning, Rose carefully turned it over. On the other side, in faded pencil, a few words were written. 'Lux in Coronum', Templecombe, Somerset. *What the heck does that mean?* she wondered.

Her mother's call interrupted her thoughts, and she replaced the frame on the wall before joining her in the kitchen.

*

"That's better," Rose said as she looked at her reflection in the antique mirror later that evening. She rearranged her curls, straightened her dress, and checked her make-up. She felt ready to face the world. She was only having a drink in Maison, but until that morning, even that had felt too overwhelming. She hadn't been out in months, not since she'd abruptly left her and Adam's apartment. Maison had always truly been Rose's safe harbour, where she was watched over by family and friends, both past and present. It felt like a good first outing.

Satisfied with her reflection, Rose left her room and went downstairs. She exited the building through the private door, and then she followed two young girls through Maison's mahogany framed glass double front doors. She smiled as she watched them stop in their tracks at the sight of sparkling pink Czech crystal chandeliers, twinkling like giant Christmas baubles. It lifted her spirits to see their faces light up.

She saw Big Frank, a regular, sat at the counter, his legs dangling as he swivelled nervously on a barstool. He was gobbling an almond croissant while flirting with Millie, the head waitress. Despite his nickname, Big Frank was unfortunately tiny, but ever hopeful. Rose smiled. *Everyone is looking for love.*

Stepping into Maison felt like stepping through a portal to the past. In her grandparents' day, craftwork was valued, and furniture, décor, and manners were elegant and refined. She could almost smell a hint of fine cigars and tobacco, reminding her of when smoking was *de regeur*, and the habit of many who passed through its doors.

Rose stopped at one of her father's prized pieces, an illuminated, antique cherry wood display cabinet filled with rows of colourful jewel-toned French macarons from Paris' L'Aduree. Her mouth watered as she scanned the list of flavours: *lavende, rose, pistache, café, fleur de l'orange, violette.*

My appetite's coming back. That's a good sign.

She spotted her dad at his favourite back corner booth, and headed in his direction. She saw him smile tentatively at her, and she managed a small one in return. She knew her unhappiness weighed heavily on him. She also sensed her father worried about who would carry on running Maison after he was gone, knowing full well that she was neither interested, nor capable. Her life certainly hadn't panned out as she or he had expected. She was grateful, however, that their relationship was strong again, cultivated with care after her turbulent teenage years.

"Hello, pumpkin. Are you okay?" he asked, taking his daughter's face gently in his hands. "What are we going to do with you, Rose? We have to get you past this."

"That's easier said than done."

"Think positively. Fake it until you make it. Isn't that what they say? Focus on the good things. Come on. Give it a try. Tell me something good about yourself."

Rose took another deep breath and sighed. "Well, I'm not too bad-looking for a woman my age, I guess."

"You're a looker! And...?"

"I've got a great family, good friends, well, a couple of good friends," she said, furrowing her brow.

"Rose, listen. This isn't easy for any of us. But nowadays, divorce is more common than not. It's nothing to be ashamed of."

Rose watched her father's attention shift to her mother, who had just entered Maison, and was behind the bar talking to Millie.

"That's easy for you to say. Your eyes still light up when

you see Mom walk into the room. Fifty years later!"

She envied her parents. They had fallen instantly in love when their eyes met at a party. Love at first sight. After a night of dance and conversation, they had never parted. Magnetism bound them together, despite the odds of a Jewish man marrying a *shiksa*.

"I thought I could have that too."

"I know. That's what we all thought." He shrugged his shoulders. "Things happen. You have to pick up the pieces. But no matter what, we're always gonna be here for you." Though his words touched her, they both knew that *always* wasn't that long for a man of his years.

Samuel winked at his wife with his hand over his heart, then he and Rose settled down into the booth. Rose picked up the menu and scanned it, even though she knew it by heart.

"Remember how you used to lay under this very table, surrounded by piles of colouring books and broken crayons?" Samuel asked. "Daddy, what's burnt sienna?" he mimicked.

"Stop!" she said half-heartedly, putting the menu down.

"Hey, remember that day you performed emergency surgery with scotch tape on my paper doll with the ripped arm?"

"How could I forget? Oh, and I have a confession. I think you're ready to handle it now."

"What?" Rose asked tentatively.

"I could see your little shoes sticking out from under the curtains when we played hide and seek. 'Ready or not, here I come!' 'Where are you? I can't find you!'" He chuckled.

"Dad!"

"I have so many treasured memories, all tucked away right here," he tapped a finger on his chest and tilted his head. "At the end of a long day, when I was in the office placing orders, your meticulous mother would be tallying the accounts, and you would be curled up in a ball on Grandpa's old recliner," Samuel's eyes glazed over. "It made it all worthwhile. Gave my life meaning. You know, Rose, you and your mother are the greatest thing that ever happened to me. I tell you all the time, but it's true. And Grandpa would have loved you to pieces." Rose lowered her gaze. She had heard so many stories of her Grandfather, and he still felt very present. His legacy was everywhere.

Samuel rubbed his hand over the shiny surface of the booth. He had fallen in love with the rich red tone of the rouge griotte marble on one of his trips to France, and although it had been a very expensive endeavour, he had changed all of the table and counter tops. Elizabeth was shocked when she'd received the invoice. He picked up the cocktail menu, a printed copy of the original from his father's era. Manhattans, whiskey sours, sidecars, champagne cocktails, and gin rickeys were having a revival.

"I recall a day, Rose, when Grandpa stood right there, next to where you're sitting. He had a highball in one hand, and an almighty fat Havana cigar clenched between his teeth. He summoned everyone over. And I mean everyone. 'Show 'em boychik' he said, patting me on the head. I must have been about five. I had this huge grin, but no front teeth. I was such a small kid, but I stood on my tiptoes, stretching until I got my chin to rest on this table top. Everyone clapped." Samuel reminisced. "I can still hear his voice now. 'My boy's growing into a fine young man'," Samuel mimicked his father in his best Russian accent. "'One day, this will be yours, my son,' he announced. He was so proud of me, Rose. The first American in the Cohen family. He made me promise to never, ever forget that America was the greatest place on earth, that anything was possible, and of that, he was proof." He looked into her eyes sadly. "With everything that is happening these days, I wonder if that is still the case."

Father and daughter were linked together by an ancestral chain to the comforting smells and tastes and history of Maison. Their souls were intimately intertwined in the common experience of a safe and contented youth.

Shaking off his sudden melancholy, Samuel handed the menu to Rose and smiled. "What'll you have?"

"Champagne cocktails!"

Samuel summoned Millie over. "Two champagne cocktails please, Millie."

"Sure thing, Mr. Cohen. Be right up."

"Shalom!" interrupted Edith Goldsmith, an elegant, commanding and dignified woman of an advanced age. She'd frequented Maison for over thirty-five years and had become part of the family.

"Shalom!" Samuel stood upon her arrival, as men of his generation did when a woman entered.

Rose wrapped her arms around Edith's shoulders and squeezed her tightly, inhaling her signature Tea Rose perfume.

"Oy vey, what a day!" Edith wiped her brow and waved her hand for Rose to scoot over.

"Tell us all about it," Rose said. "Champagne cocktail?"

"At this time of day? You should be ashamed to ask an old woman such a thing! It would finish me off. I'll have Earl Grey tea."

Samuel suddenly sat upright as if in the presence of royal company. "Your Majesty, may I suggest some biscuits with your tea?" he asked, affecting an English accent.

Edith blushed coyly. "Oh, no thank you. *We* don't eat biscuits. Only crumpets." They both giggled like children, only stopping when Millie arrived with their order.

The head waitress set two champagne flutes on the table, popped the cork, then carefully poured the frothing liquid over sugar cubes, bitters, and cognac, creating a fountain of bubbles.

Rose quickly slurped the foam, then raised her glass.

"What are we celebrating?" asked Samuel.

"I've got something to celebrate!" Edith said excitedly. "Ananda is coming to New York!"

"That orange robed Hare Krishna you're always on

about?" Samuel mocked.

"Save the sarcasm, Samuel Cohen," Edith said, gently slapping his hand.

"Sorry, Edith," he answered sheepishly. "Truth be told, I've witnessed tremendous changes in you since, wait, what's his name?"

"Ananda."

"Oh yes, Ananda. You know, I think I'd like to meet this Ananda, check him out while he's here."

"Mazel Tov, the miracles have already begun." Edith took his hand again, and kissed the back of it. "Samuel Cohen, you've made my day."

Rose contemplated her father's remarks to Edith. Fate had dealt Edith a horrible blow, cruelly taking her husband and then her daughter shortly after. She had been in a terrible state for years, until the holy man had crossed her path in India.

"That's wonderful, Edith! After all these years! Where's he staying? Do you need help? I can put leaflets out if he is doing an event."

"Slow down! One question at a time. Kids," she tutted. "Can't keep up with them."

"I'm hardly a kid," Rose retorted.

"My dear, Rose, you'll always be a kid to me," Edith replied.

"And me," Samuel added.

"I appreciate the offer, but no leafleting is needed. And he'll be staying at my house. What was your other question? Oh, yes, for how long? I'm not sure," Edith said with a shrug of her shoulders.

"Edith, tell me, how did you persuade Ananda to come? You've been trying for years," Rose asked, finishing the last half of her cocktail, and filling her glass again.

Edith raised her brow.

"I didn't persuade him, honey. He always said he would come when the time was right. Last week, I received an email from Richard, one of his closest English speaking disciples, I mean, associates."

Disciples? That's gonna put Dad right off, Rose thought.

"Richard's been living in the ashram for years. We talked about bringing Ananda over several times." Edith smiled. "They arrive this Friday! I have to keep pinching myself. Oh! By the way, I'm having a private gathering over the weekend. We'll see you there?"

"You haven't given yourself much time to prepare," Rose said.

"I've been preparing for a very long time. I really would like the whole family to come," Edith added.

"Dad and I will be there. Right?"

"Of course we will. Wouldn't want to get on the wrong side of you two!"

"I can't wait," added Rose. "But Mom probably won't come. She's not very open to this sort of thing."

Samuel pursed his lips, nodding in agreement.

An unexpected shiver ran up Rose's spine. She had enjoyed hearing about Edith's journey with Ananda in the past, but now the master was stepping out of the stories and into her life. She felt nervous and excited, and had a strong feeling that after meeting him, nothing in her life would remain the same.

CHAPTER 3

EDOUARD RENE DE LABOULAYE
The Masonic Lodge, Paris
1865

On the outskirts of Versailles, a group of noble men, Freemasons of the highest degree, gathered for dinner at the home of Edouard René de Laboulaye. Edouard was an expert on the American Constitution, an interpreter of law, and an anti-slavery activist. Unbeknownst to all but a few, he was also a psychic channel. On this fateful night, Edouard would present his brothers with an idea that would change the course of history.

Guests in attendance included Oscar and Edmond de Lafayette, grandsons of the Marquis (Masonic brother of George Washington), Historian Henri Martin, artist Frédéric Auguste Bartholdi, and Stonemason Richard Duchêne. All were pure of heart, humble, honourable, ethical, and committed to being of service to humanity.

The sommelier poured a sample of an 1812 Chateaux Laffite, while Monsieur Laboulaye addressed his guests.

"Gentlemen. Thank you for coming at such short notice. We are gathered this evening to enjoy the bounty of our land and sea, and something perhaps even greater still, which will fill our souls as well as our bellies."

He swished a sip of wine around his palate and spat it into a vessel, nodding with approval. Edouard raised his glass, and gestured for the wine to be poured for his guests.

"As you all know, over the years, I've been fortunate to receive guidance and instruction for our lodge regarding various important matters, through surrendering myself to the process of automatic writing."

He waved a rolled parchment in the air.

"My dear brothers. My friends. At two o'clock this morning, I was prompted to get out of my bed. After what felt like hours of struggle, a breakthrough came. What you are about to hear may astound you. I can tell you, I am truly astonished myself."

As Edouard spoke, he noticed a light filling the corner of the room. It was a familiar presence that often came when they gathered. It was a signal for them to pay attention because what was being presented was ordained. He saw that his guests, too, witnessed the divine light. They set their wine glasses on the table, acknowledged it, and then focused back on him. Adjusting his spectacles, he slid the candelabra closer, dripping wax all over the linen table cloth.

"We have been brought together by a common fate, each of us an integral spoke on the wheel of destiny. We have been given a mission through a message passed on from mystical guardians working behind the scenes of the earth's spiritual unfolding. Gentleman, we have been given instructions to present America with a gift, a monument, honouring the freedom that was won, and the spiritual freedom that will take root in the country and spread across the globe."

Excitement and chatter filled the room. Edouard tapped his wine glass with a silver spoon.

"What more can you tell us?" Richard Duchene pleaded.

"I cannot tell you how, or what. I can only say that the process has begun. There will be six years of preparation. I am assured that we will be guided at every step. I shall now read the instruction, which I received clearly, word for word." He unrolled the parchment. "'There will be difficulties. Your country is in political turmoil. What is being played out on the world stage will be distressing. Remember to have faith and hold true to the teaching and foundation of your lodge. God's Kingdom is perfect and is being established on the earth.'" Edouard set down the parchment, and looked around the men sat at the table. "Well, there you have it."

One by one, the men stood, and put their hand solemnly to their heart. They then touched their fists together in the centre, their arms becoming spokes on a wheel, and turned in a circle. This was a ritual, an oath signifying unity and an acknowledgement that each was in alignment with the higher cause, and would willingly, and wholeheartedly, participate in facilitating it. Their commitment to serve had gifted them with a great responsibility.

*

Edouard couldn't sleep that night. He lay awake thinking about his order of the lodge, and how unlike other lodges and esoteric brotherhoods it was. Its secrets, codes, and rituals were handed down through a lineage that could be traced back to Moses. He reflected on Moses leading his people out of slavery, and how similar and desperate the cries of the French were now. He hoped the gift to America would inspire the people of France to fight for their own democracy.

After continuing to toss and turn in bed for some time, Edouard felt guided to sit at his desk and see if anything else was waiting to come through.

Before he sat, he lit a candle. With his arms out and palms face up, he turned clockwise three times, surrendering his ego and personal will, opening himself up as an instrument of divine service. He always performed this ritual before sitting at the roll-top desk to receive information from the higher realms through his writing. He sat down. The candle flickered. He set out a parchment, quill, and inkwell.

He closed his eyes. After a moment, a warm glow filled his body, and the familiar presence entered the room. When he opened his eyes, something beyond him picked up the quill and dipped it into the inkwell, using his body as its instrument. His hand moved across the parchment at tremendous speed, until the ink ran dry and the tip scratched the surface. His arm moved again, at its own volition, back to the inkwell. Finally, the hand stopped writing, and felt like his own again.

After waiting a few minutes for the ink to dry, he lifted the parchment to the light. Edouard was never conscious of what was written, until he read it to himself.

"I answered the prayers and cries for freedom of the Israelites, through my beloved son, Moses, who was given the revelation of the Ten Commandments. I taught him how to imbue matter with spiritual essence, through the Archangels Michael and Gabriel, and so the new laws of the new land were put into the tablets of stone, which were a tangible, physical manifestation of higher consciousness. And then to protect and transport, I gave precise instruction on how to build the Ark of the Covenant."

Edouard looked towards the heavens. "Mon dieu. Have you really spoken directly to me?" He was in shock. It took a lot of concentration to read and absorb what was written next, but after some scrutiny, he deciphered the scrawl, which was clearly a reference to a passage in the bible.

Pulling a leather-bound bible from his bookshelf, he flipped through the pages until he reached the passage in the Book of Exodus 35:

'And he hath filled him with the spirit of God, in wisdom, in understanding, and in knowledge, and in all manner of workmanship; And to devise curious works, to work in gold, and in silver, and in brass, And in the cutting of stones, to set [them], and in carving of wood, to make any manner of cunning work. And he hath put in his heart that he may teach, [both] he, and Aholiab, the son of Ahisamach, of the

tribe of Dan. Them hath he filled with wisdom of heart, to work all manner of work, of the engraver, and of the cunning workman, and of the embroiderer, in blue, and in purple, in scarlet, and in fine linen, and of the weaver, [even] of them that do any work, and of those that devise cunning work. Then wrought Bezaleel and Aholiab, and every wise hearted man, in whom the LORD put wisdom and understanding to know how to work all manner of work for the service of the sanctuary, according to all that the LORD had commanded.'

He lay down on his bed, wondering what relevance the passage bore to him or the lodge. Did it have something to do with the gift they'd been requested to bequeath to America?

CHAPTER 4

EDITH GOLDSMITH
New York City
Present Day

Edith woke early before the alarm, too early to get up and prepare breakfast. She didn't want to wake her guests. She lay in bed for a while, thinking about the day ahead. After some time, she slipped a dressing gown on over her night gown and quietly made her way to the kitchen. When she stepped through the door, she was startled by a man's voice.

"Good morning, Edith. Hope you don't mind," Richard said, raising his mug from where he sat at the breakfast bar.

"Richard! You startled me!" She stopped in her tracks, put her hand on her chest, and pulled her pink robe more tightly around her. Her face flushed. *I'm such an old fool. I should've gotten dressed first.* "No, not at all. Of course not. How long have you been up? I didn't expect to see you for at least another hour or two."

"Not long. Just enough time to make a pot of coffee."

"Did you sleep okay?"

"Very well, thank you. I forgot how nice it is to sleep on such a plush mattress. I could get used to it."

"Enjoy it while it lasts," Edith said with a chuckle, knowing personally that life on the ashram was far from decadent. Her eyes scanned Richard from head to toe. *That won't do,* Edith thought, frowning at his scruffy t-shirt and jeans. *Maybe in San Francisco...*

"Good morning."

Edith looked up to see Ananda stood in front of her, all dressed and ready, in slacks and a shirt instead of in his customary white robe.

"Good morning, Ananda," Richard and Edith said in unison. Richard went to Ananda and touched his feet. Ananda placed his hand on Richard's head.

"Please sit," he said, placing his hand on his heart. "It is a joy to finally be in your beautiful country."

"Please excuse me," Edith muttered, mortified that she wasn't yet presentable. "Richard, would you mind getting Ananda something hot to drink?" she asked before she scurried back to her room. "I'll only be a moment."

*

"You must be starved after your travels," Edith said when she finally returned, smiling graciously. She quickly set the table, then scampered back and forth with breakfast items: a jug of orange juice, a tray of bagels, cream cheese, tomatoes, and onions. "I thought you might like to try some of *our* traditional food."

"This looks very delicious, Edith. And I must say, you look lovely as well."

Edith touched her perfectly coiffed hair and smoothed her smart dress over her hip, blushing a little. No one had seen her in such an intimate way since her husband had passed. Her teacher seeing her looking so dishevelled was almost unbearable, especially as he was from such a traditional culture. But he seemed unfazed, like he hadn't even noticed.

"Let us please take a moment to give thanks before enjoying this wonderful meal."

Edith watched Ananda chant a Sanskrit blessing over the food, and felt very blessed at having this special private time in his presence.

"Don't New Yorkers normally have salmon with bagels?" Ananda asked.

"Yes, but, aren't you vegetarian?" replied Edith.

Ananda pointed to the fridge. "Yes *I* am."

On the way to the kitchen, she thought about the vegetarian diet at the ashram, and how happy she had been to partake – she had even looked forward to it. She had never ever felt hungry or deprived. It suited her, and she'd always returned home with more energy, and less aches and pains. Recently, meat and fish had become a diminishing part of her diet, without effort or thought. Why then, didn't she adopt it fully into her lifestyle? She carefully unwrapped the white paper, but the soft pink flesh that she'd bought fresh from the local deli, which was part of her cultural heritage, was losing its appeal. She didn't feel right eating it around her teacher. The message was clear. It was time. She returned to the table empty-handed. "I'm going to give it to the neighbour's cat," she announced.

Ananda inclined his head slightly and smiled.

She offered the tray to Ananda first, who stared at the selection. He pointed to a poppy seed bagel. Edith carefully picked it up with tongs and put it on his plate. She then turned to Richard.

"That one."

"Good choice," Edith said, placing the 'everything' bagel on his plate.

After pouring fresh orange juice from the farmer's market, and generally fussing over them, she finally turned her attention to her own food. Ananda watched as she took a bagel, expertly sliced it, and slathered cream cheese on both sides. He copied her and did the same. Ananda was mindful as he ate, taking his time over each bite, savouring the tastes and textures. Edith attempted to chew at his pace, which felt as unnatural to her as the lack of conversation.

Ananda finished eating, wiped his mouth, and set his

napkin on the table. "Very nice. I like the poppy seeds."

"Have you two made any plans?" Edith asked, dabbing a napkin at the corners of her mouth, relieved the silence was broken.

"We were hoping to see a bit of the city today," Richard answered, tucking into his second bagel, which he ate sandwich-style, filled with mounds of cream cheese, onions and tomato. "Maybe you can show us around? If there's time," he added, before taking a large bite. Edith was delighted with his enthusiasm. She was starting to have a soft spot for Richard. He felt like a son. She pointed to her upper lip, indicating to him that there was a blob of cream cheese on his face. He smiled and wiped his mouth with his napkin while he chewed.

"I'm at your service. Is there anywhere special you'd like me to take you? There's so much to see."

Ananda's eyes lit up. "I would very much like to visit the Lady Liberty today. I've wanted to go from the time I was a little boy. I have seen so many pictures."

Edith's heart sank. She hadn't planned on such a complicated excursion. She had hoped for something like a walk to Central Park and a museum visit. "It would be my pleasure to take you there, Ananda. I haven't been for many years." Edith paused. "Though we must be back in enough time to prepare for this evening."

"Of course. No worries. There is plenty of time, Edith," Ananda said reassuringly.

Edith, however, wasn't so sure. As a meticulous organiser and efficient timekeeper, she felt she was out of her comfort zone. She was worried that she would be as unprepared for the evening meeting as she was for her guests that morning.

After breakfast, Edith cleared up, and walked slowly past Ananda's room. The door was slightly ajar, and offered just enough scope to sneak a peek without feeling like she was spying. The bed was still made. *Has he even slept in it?* She opened the door a little further, looked back towards the dining room to make sure no one was coming, and stuck her head in. A rolled grass mat and small neck pillow were neatly tucked near the bureau. She breathed deeply, a palpable vibration of divine presence permeated her being like a breath of fresh air.

*

"Ooh, you're so handsome, Thomas," Edith said, pinching the doorman's cheeks, as she so often did when she was in a good mood.

"Good morning, Mrs Goldsmith. You're not so bad yourself," he answered, rubbing his sore face.

"Not so bad for an old lady, eh?"

"No, Mrs Goldsmith. Not bad at all," Thomas smiled, opening the door for Edith and her guests.

The early summer morning could not have been more beautiful. A storm in the middle of the night had provided relief from the customary oppressive humidity, and along with a clear blue sky, it was the perfect welcome to Manhattan. Ananda turned his face towards the sun and took a deep breath. Thomas stepped off the curb to wave down a yellow cab.

"A taxi?" Ananda looked to Edith. "Let's go by subway!"

"Okay, subway it is," Edith agreed with a shrug. "Thomas," she called. "Tell me, do you know how to get to the Statue of Liberty? We're going underground."

"Do I ever. Take the number 4 train on Park to Battery. Then walk to Clinton Castle. Be sure to purchase your ferry and museum tickets there. It's only a short ten-minute boat ride. Here, wait, you'll need this." He ran inside and grabbed a city map from behind the counter. "Are you sure, Mister?" he said to Ananda as he handed him the map. "The subway can get really crowded this time of day. And smelly."

"Have you ever been on a train in India, my friend?"

"Can't say I have."

"We'll be fine. If it's full, we can always find a place on the roof!"

Ananda's feet barely touched the ground as he strode with a youthful exuberance down the sidewalk like an excited schoolboy on a fieldtrip. "A far cry from Mumbai!"

The traffic slowed and came to a halt alongside them. A cabbie flicked a cigarette butt onto the sidewalk with his thumb and forefinger, then stuck his head out the window. "Hey, what's goin' on up there?" he demanded. More horns and more shouting followed.

Ananda covered his ears. "Maybe not so different from Mumbai after all!"

"Stay close, and hold your belongings tight," Edith said, when they reached the entrance to the station. Holding onto the railing, she led them down the stairs, through the crowd, and pushed her way towards the train about to leave the platform.

"Stop," Ananda said over the din. "No need to rush, even though it's 'rush' hour. Time is a funny thing. If you let go, it will always work in your favour."

Edith found it a bit ironic, considering Ananda's sprint down Park Avenue, but it seemed he was right. They managed to get on at the last second, and even found seats.

"Thanks to Lord Ganesh!" Ananda exclaimed.

The train jerked side to side like a rickety wooden roller coaster as it made its way through the underground labyrinth. At the next stop, an aggressive-looking young man boarded, and shoved his way through the crowd. Edith clutched her bag closer. He stopped for a second, standing right in front of her seat. Her heart jumped and skipped a beat, as she averted her gaze from his. She felt immediately uncomfortable, threatened even. With his tattoos and piercings, and stench of tobacco and sweat, he seemed dangerous. This is why she made a point of avoiding the subway.

She breathed a sigh of relief as he moved away. People recoiled as he progressed down the subway car. He knocked into several travellers, quite unapologetically, as the train bumped and lurched down the track. "Well, move over then!" he grumbled, in a thick accent, jabbing his elbow into an elderly gentleman who didn't move away quickly enough.

Ananda rose from his seat opposite Edith, and beckoned the young man back over. He turned around, and walked towards them.

"What are you doing?" Edith hissed. "This is dangerous."

Ananda signalled to Edith with his hand, asking her to be still.

The young punk swaggered over to Ananda, and got in his face.

"Yeah, so what's the problem, chief?"

Ananda stepped back a little, completely unfazed. He gestured to his vacant seat. "Please, sir, sit down. Have my seat."

"Yo, for real, man? Get outtah here," the punk said, turning away from Ananda, waving him off dismissively.

Ananda reached out and took hold of the young man's hand.

Edith's mind was going crazy. She was overcome with fear. *He's out of his depth. He doesn't know about the gang culture*, she thought. *I should have warned him. That man could have a knife, or worse, a gun, and he probably isn't afraid to use it.* Grim scenarios raced through her mind as she sat frozen with terror.

"Yo, get off me, man!" the punk shouted, pulling his hand away and pushing Ananda violently backwards, slamming him into Edith.

"Oh my goodness!" Edith cried.

The punk slumped down in the seat vacated by Ananda, shaking his head at what had just happened.

Ananda got up, apologized to Edith, steadied himself and

walked back over to the man. At this point, Richard stood up to go to his teacher's assistance. Ananda waved him back, and sat down beside the man, who unsurprisingly had open seats on either side of him now, as people had moved away, fearing that a fight was about to break out.

Ananda took the punk's hand again, with a grip so firm he was helpless to break free. After a momentary struggle, the young man gave up, but refused to look at Ananda. "Yo, man, for real. Can you just let me go?" he said, sounding bored and tired.

Edith's heart was racing as she watched the two men. She really hoped Ananda knew what he was doing.

"You know, man, I gotta get off in a couple of stops. What's your problem? Enough already!"

The young man turned slightly and caught Ananda's gaze.

"Please, Mister," his voice had been reduced to a whimper.

But Ananda kept a tight grip.

Lowering his head in frustration, with no choice but to surrender, he slumped back in the seat.

Ananda loosened his grip and leaned in, putting his hand on the young man's shoulder.

"I know it has been tough for you since your mother died. You were fourteen. You found her, right? You were placed in an orphanage, and then foster homes, but you always ran away," Ananda said. The punk's head snapped around and he looked deeply into the Swami's eyes.

"Your father left two years earlier, when you were twelve."

"Please, Mister," the punk whispered.

"Until then, you were devout, like your mother. In fact, you were destined for the church, but circumstances changed, and you took another path," Ananda continued.

"My God," the young man said, covering his face with both hands. "You are like my grandmother, *mi abuela*, she could tell me things too."

"Yes, my son. Remember, just before your grandmother died, she told you that you had a choice. You chose the life of thievery and drug use."

Ananda gently took the man's hand in his again. That was all it took. The young man was stoic, but the tears that streamed down his face betrayed his composure.

A few people looked away, as if not wanting to intrude on such a private moment. Edith sat shaking her head, feeling forlorn, and perhaps even a bit angry with herself.

"Today," Ananda continued, "another opportunity steps in. Think back. A couple of months ago, you reached out. Do you remember?"

The young man's thoughts instantly flashed to a day, not long ago, at St. Patrick's cathedral. He had lost his will to live. It was the first time he'd gone into a church in years. He wasn't even sure why he was there, except he thought perhaps he should give one last attempt to make peace with a creator he wasn't even sure he believed in. Sliding into a pew towards the front, he stared at Jesus on the cross, and lowered his head into his hands on the pew in front of him. Tears dripped down his nose and chin, dropping onto the floor below. He contemplated how lonely and hopeless his life felt. While wiping his tears with the back of his leather jacket, he noticed a string of Rosary beads just like the one his mother used on the floor at his feet. Her rosary had been misplaced in the confusion following her death. He could not recall many days in his life, nor did he care to, but that day was etched in his psyche. For a split second he thought that maybe, just maybe, his mother's spirit had left the beads for him. He quickly dismissed the possibility. He was hungry, and angry that he was alive and his mother wasn't. He put the rosary beads in his pocket intending to sell them. On the way out of the cathedral, a young woman handed him a ten dollar bill. "Go and get some lunch," she had said.

The young man nodded, clearly lost in thought. Tears

streamed faster down his cheeks.

Edith knew that she was witnessing a miracle, and felt ashamed she had briefly forgotten that the man who stood before her was the incredible teacher she had found in India. His western attire and childlike attitude had masked his true power. Her thoughts turned to the *A Course in Miracles* discourse on judging by appearances, and how to look with the inner eye. Today, Edith had failed these teachings on two accounts. The young man she'd had such an extreme reaction to, was vulnerable, and had a sweet nature that had remained hidden on first sight. He was not without a soul, a story, a history. Her immediate fear of him, while well warranted, made her angry with herself now. She wondered how receiving these kinds of reactions, on a daily basis, had conditioned him to see himself. And how dare she question Ananda, instead of support him? Hadn't he saved her very own life? It was never about the robe, or the rituals, or the ashram, or devotees; it was only about the consciousness Ananda carried. She had witnessed a true miracle, and had done many times before. She wondered if Ananda knew all along why he had to take the subway this morning.

The train arrived at Battery Park.

"Come now with us," Ananda said to the young man. "What is your name?"

"Miguel."

As they exited the subway, there was a small group handing out leaflets and taking collections for the Salvation Army.

"Who are those people?" Ananda asked.

"A Christian organisation that works with the homeless," Edith answered.

His hand on Miguel's arm, Ananda guided him over. Edith and Richard followed.

"Richard, please donate to the collection bucket, and ask if they would help Miguel get back on his feet."

One of the men nodded to Miguel as they approached.

"I've seen you at the food bank, haven't I?"

"Yeah. You have," Miguel hung his head.

"Please, look after my friend," Ananda said to the missionary holding a large bell. "And do not worry, my dear, dear, Miguel. Our paths will cross again."

CHAPTER 5

RICHARD DUNNE
Statue of Liberty, New York City
Present Day

Richard watched Edith holding on tightly to the rail, bracing herself as the ferry lilted from side to side, and the wind whipped through her no longer perfectly coiffed hair. The sun had disappeared and it was beginning to rain. She closed her eyes as the boat ebbed and dipped.

"Imagine coming all the way across the Atlantic on a sea like this," she shouted to Ananda and Richard over the rush.

Edith checked her watch several times while they waited in line to get into Liberty. She dug through her purse, retrieved a Moleskine notepad, and studied her 'to do' list.

"Relax," Richard said, sensing her worry.

"Everything is in perfect time, and everything is always perfect," Ananda reminded Edith again. "I have been waiting a very long time for this day. She has too," he added quietly.

When they were finally admitted, they stood silently for several moments, admiring a life size replica of Liberty's face, which greeted them at the entrance to the museum. Its presence immediately set a tone of gravitas, juxtaposed to the hectic and somewhat frenetic journey there.

"I didn't know Eiffel had a part in building this," Richard, said pointing to miniature of the statue's skeletal framework on display.

"Look here." Edith summoned the two men to a wall with pictures of the key Frenchmen involved in the monument's conception, design, and construction. In her best French accent, she read the list of names: "Edouard René de Laboulaye, Frédéric Auguste Bartholdi, Gustave Eiffel, Richard Morris Hunt, and Richard Duchene."

Richard glanced at the photographs and nodded, but turned his attention to a glass cabinet at the other side. It was as if a magnetic force was drawing him towards it. Suddenly feeling warm, he wiped sweat off his forehead, and pulled his shirt away from his body to let some air flow in, as he admired a set of some original tools.

Edith followed closely behind. "Are you ok? You look a little green," she said, putting a comforting hand on his arm.

"Yes, fine, I think. Hope I didn't pick something up on the plane. Feeling a little funny."

"Probably just a bit seasick," Edith assured him. "I'm sure it's nothing of concern."

"I'm sure you're right."

Ananda lightly ushered them both to a bronze replica of Liberty's foot. He put his hands together, bowed towards the foot, and touched it as if she were a Hindu God. "In Hinduism it is appropriate to touch the feet of deity to show respect." Edith turned towards Richard, looking slightly confused. He held his hands up, in a 'beats me' gesture, and walked over to a bronze plaque. A tour guide dressed in early 19th century costume joined him in reading a poem called *The New Colossus*. He stepped aside, as she recited its most famous and epic last stanza.

"Give me your tired, your poor,
Your huddled masses yearning to breathe free,
The wretched refuse of your teeming shore.
Send these, the homeless, tempest-tossed to me,
I lift my lamp beside the golden door!"

The words hit him deeply. She'd read them with such conviction and spirit. He thought of Miguel and then of his own spiritual journey. There was synchronicity in meeting the homeless, poor, and "tempest-tossed" Miguel, on the way to Liberty. It seemed like more than a coincidence, kismet almost.

"I've heard this before, maybe at school," Richard said to the guide.

"Yes. You would have. It was written by a Jewish woman, right here in New York. Emma Lazarus. It was intended to sound as if the statue herself were speaking."

"It sure is moving. I wonder why it's called *'The New Colossus'.*"

"Well," the guide explained. "*Colossus* means something of enormous importance. However, the origin of that word is Greek. *Kollossos* was used by Herodotus to describe the statues at the Egyptian temples. The poet chose the word because she believed it triggered emotions while moving through the space. *This* magical space, the Statue of Liberty."

"Yes, I do feel power here," Richard agreed, but the guide was gone.

Edith and Ananda came over. "Did you see that woman in period costume?" Richard asked, feeling puzzled.

"No," Edith said, looking around, "I didn't see anyone, and I was just a few feet away."

"Huh?" Richard lost his words as he pointed to a picture that hung on the wall nearby. "That's her!"

"That was the guide?" Edith asked, looking at him strangely. "Emma Lazarus. 1849-1887. I don't think so, Richard. She's been dead for over a century!"

*

Ananda climbed the stairs effortlessly. Edith struggled, which was to be expected. Richard, a fit man in his prime, was challenged. He dragged himself up each step to the observation deck. When they arrived, his chest was heaving.

They followed Ananda around, absorbing his spiritual nectar, like bees to a flower. They hovered as he stopped at different points to take in the awesome panoramic views of Brooklyn, New Jersey, and Manhattan.

At one point, Ananda stopped, shut his eyes, and remained perfectly still, as still as the statue herself. Seemingly unaware of the activity around him, he remained on the spot for about five minutes. Richard and Edith flanked him silently, absorbing a peaceful, yet charged energy. After some time, his lips curved into a satisfied smile, and he continued on.

"One for the memory books?" Edith said, holding up her camera. Ananda and Richard stood side by side, against the backdrop of the entry into America from the Atlantic. Ananda waved her over to join them, pulling a smartphone out of his pocket. "How about a selfie?"

They had just snapped a few photos when Edith noticed something in the image behind them. She turned to look.

"A rainbow!" Edith shouted over gusts of wind.

"Ah, beautiful. God's blessing is upon us," Ananda observed.

"Wow, isn't she powerful?" Richard said in awe of the statue.

"Of course she is! She's a goddess!" exclaimed Edith.

"Yes," said Ananda. "Libertas. Roman. The Goddess of freedom. We've come through the age of reason, and we are now entering the age of freedom. But not necessarily how you might think of it." His demeanour became serious and thoughtful. "Thank you, Edith. Thank you, Richard. I was meant to come here today, to physically experience the Statue of Liberty. Tonight, during my meditation, I will go into the monument's inner meaning. It is a profound place, almost ready to fulfil its true ancient and original purpose." Ananda looked around. "It is multi-dimensional. It is a holy place, blessed since the beginning."

Richard and Edith hung on his words.

"Just as she physically has different levels, the star base, the pedestal, the body, the crown, and torch, she also has different levels of symbolic and esoteric meaning. It is a mystical place. You will see. Many will come here in the future, on pilgrimage, to work at the deeper levels." As if snapping himself out of a kind of channelling, Ananda clapped his hands together. "For now, let's just experience."

Edith broke the long silence that proceeded Ananda's insights. "It's getting late, we should get back soon."

"Back? We've only just begun. Onwards and upwards!" Ananda commanded, with his arm raised and his forefinger pointing to the sky. "We are going all the way."

Edith looked at her watch. "One-thirty. Still time."

The stairs became increasingly narrow at each level. Richard disliked enclosed spaces, and heights for that matter. He'd once got stuck in a glass elevator at the top floor of a new shopping mall in San Francisco. Even though it was only for a few minutes, it had felt like eternity. He thought the elevator might fall, or that there would be an earthquake or a fire.

He paused for a breath on the stairs, and contemplated waiting at the bottom for Edith and Ananda, but he could feel Ananda's insistence, and after years of spending time at his side, he recognized when a major spiritual teaching was unfolding, either for himself, or for those in their company. He had a strong suspicion this teaching was coming for him.

Richard's feet felt heavy as he dragged himself up the stairs after his companions. It was the same weightiness he often felt when walking through the tunnel to board an airplane. He was so frightened of flying; it was as if his body were fighting him to stay earthbound. He remembered Ananda's instruction to chant his mantra always, especially when his mind was out of control. Inwardly, he recited the four sacred Sanskrit words that connected him to Ananda through time and space. Each word carried him up a step.

Ananda reached into his pocket and passed something to Richard. A candy, *prasad* from his teacher, was a blessing more precious than gold. Richard knew it contained all he would need to move through his fears. He popped it in his mouth, and continued towards the crown. As the last bit of strawberry hard candy melted on his tongue, a series of images appeared in sudden vision. A warehouse, the French flag, a group of men toiling. One big man with strong hands looked up and stared straight through Richard.

It's me! Richard thought with a gasp. Then he saw the Roman numerals 1776, being chiselled onto a stone tablet. Then he could actually hear the men. One of them spoke in French, *"Lorsque le moment est venu, tout sera révélé."*

Richard understood what they were saying, even though he didn't speak a word of the language.

When the time is right, all will be revealed.

"Quicker, Mom!" a little girl behind Richard demanded of her mother. Eager to get to the top, she accidentally stood on Richard's heel, pulling his shoe off, and knocking him out of his vision. Richard lost his balance, along with a bit of his temper, and shot the little girl an angry look. He was not proud of his loss of control.

He had been doing a specific meditation with Ananda for some time to awaken the *kundalini*, known as the sleeping serpent. He'd had several experiences of energy moving up his spine, some were almost orgasmic, but this was the first time he'd had an actual vision, a sign that his third eye was opening. Recalling his own impatience for enlightenment after committing to stay at the ashram, he was able to find some compassion for the little girl, but it was too late to show it, as she had pushed past with her mother and moved on ahead.

Ananda had told him it would be a long process, and that perseverance was required. After their first meeting when Ananda had told him to stay, he didn't have another private meeting for an entire year. Learning patience had become a major part of Richard's journey.

Richard gripped the rail and concentrated on putting one foot in front of the other, counting each step, saying his mantra, surrendering to the tight space, the inability to get out if needed, and the impatience of the little girl. He chose to trust, to remain present in the moment, and aware that life had taken him to the foot of a great teacher, and that things had never been the same since. For how many lifetimes had he followed this soul that he called his teacher? A warm glow filled his heart. He wiped away a tear of gratitude that trickled down his cheek, but they kept coming, etching a pathway down the side of his face. He hid them from those around him, embarrassed at his loss of control.

"True power is vulnerability." He heard Ananda's voice repeat the words he'd heard over and over, but never consciously embodied. Step by step, he ascended, contemplating his vulnerability. Another vision came. This time of the fighting and the break-up of his marriage. He felt a tremendous pain in his solar plexus from the rejection he'd felt when Mandy had left him. He confronted his relentless need to control the relationship. Even though he knew it wasn't right, he couldn't stop. He remembered his father's domineering mannerisms, and realised how they had both subjugated the feminine.

They finally arrived at the double helix staircase, the final ascent to the crown of Lady Liberty.

"No turning back now!" Richard asserted.

"Look forward," Edith ordered. "It's a long way down! And up! Is everybody ready?"

"Ready," Ananda confirmed.

Richard observed the structural metal framework, like the miniature he'd seen in the museum, designed by Gustave Eiffel, the maker of the Eiffel Tower in Paris. *It's like a skeleton, and the copper is like skin.*

When they finally reached the top, Ananda took their hands in his. "Please. Close your eyes for a moment. Take in the energy."

Richard felt a charge going through him, from Ananda's hand. "You are now standing on the most important spot on earth."

Richard knew he'd been going through an important inner process from the start. There were so many questions, but the time wasn't right.

"Tonight at the gathering, I will go into the fullness of this sacred site," Ananda said. "And I will explain why we had to come here. For now, enjoy." At that moment, the little girl and her mother squeezed by them, breaking the spell.

They took a final look out the window, across the horizon, up towards the golden torch, and down towards the tablet. The stone tablet that Richard had seen in his vision.

CHAPTER 6

EDOUARD RENE DE LABOULAYE
The Masonic Lodge, Paris
Paris, 1871

Hidden in plain sight on one of Paris's oldest streets, on la rue Saint-Séverin, close to the Church Saint-Séverin, was the grand lodge. To the untrained eye, it looked like nothing special. The building's fascia was narrow, but its true girth was sequestered behind the commercial space, which operated as a humble shelter for pilgrims going to the church and Notre Dame. A perfect façade for the important matters that were really going on. Once inside the back chambers, a world of opulence and intrigue awaited.

Six years had lapsed before the next piece of the puzzle was revealed, as was prophesized. The men arrived within minutes of each other, passing through the establishment, with a nod to its owner, before proceeding down a cramped hallway, through a warren of rooms, passageways and corridors. When they reached a mahogany panelled wall, they gave the secret knock, gaining admittance through an arched door, which swung inward, allowing them entry to the meeting room.

It was pitch dark, except for a beam of light which pierced through a stained glass window at the centre of a domed ceiling. The window, surrounded by painted astrological constellations on a midnight sky, illuminated a miniature model of Solomon's Temple, which was situated carefully in the centre of the black and white checkered floor, which symbolised light and dark. On the wall hung symbols of the lodge and trade: a square and compass, a phoenix, an anchor, and a wheel.

The men stood in a circle, dressed in seamless white robes like those of the original mason, Moses, who as a true servant of God didn't wear priestly garb, which separated him from the masses.

Edouard Rene de Laboulaye held an acacia wood box, containing a white candle, which had been blessed with oils of amber, frankincense and rose, and consecrated with intent and prayer. He set it on the altar, broke a match off the comb, and pulled it quickly between doubled over sandpaper, igniting a flame. Then he took the candle to each man, who in turn faced their left palm up towards heaven, circled their right hand six inches above the flame, before placing it slowly over their heart.

"Do you offer your heart, mind and body in divine service to the one?" Laboulaye asked.

"I offer myself in divine service in heart, mind and body," each answered. Laboulaye then placed the candle into the miniature temple in the centre of the room. It remained there throughout the meeting, representing the enlightened soul and the connection between heaven and earth. Edouard addressed the group.

"Dear Brothers, it has been a long time since we have gathered. Each of us has faced challenges, and tests, in preparation for this holy night. The trials that we have endured over the past years have been in alignment with the particular roles that each will play in the next phase of creating our offering to the United States."

"Here, here," the men said in unison.

"During the night after we first gathered, all those years ago, I was prompted to channel again, and was led to a passage in the Bible. At the time, I wasn't sure of its significance to us, or if it had any, however, after much contemplation, illumination came. Alas, I must trust my inner guidance. The passage was from Exodus, which spoke of God's chosen men, the humble and pure of heart, who with childlike innocence and lack of ego, were selected to build the Ark of the Covenant. God designated the gifted and skilled artist Bezaleel." He looked towards Bartholdi.

"My dear Frederic, the visionary artist, your adult life has consisted of travelling Europe, studying classical architecture and artistic symbolism. You have even visited the great pyramids in Egypt, unknowingly cultivating your connection with the over-soul of our project, guided since the beginning. The time has come to propose this contribution to America, and you, my friend, have been chosen to design it. I truly believe this is a command from on high. Dear Brother, will you accept this bequest?"

Edouard's words resonated deeply within Bartholdi; he felt it in every fibre of his being. He placed his hand over his heart and bowed towards the candle. "With gratitude, I humbly accept this mission. But what is it, may I ask?"

"You will receive inspiration when the time is right. It is in your hands. Trust," Laboulaye insisted. He turned to his dear and principled friend, Henri Martin. "Henri, the task of raising the initial funds to get the project started lies in your hands. As a man who is greatly respected in the community, you can rally the support."

"It would be my honour," Henri replied.

"The gift shall be presented on July 4th 1886, marking the hundredth anniversary of the Declaration of Independence, and the country's freedom from British Rule."

The candle flickered erratically, although the room was still, prompting the men to stop talking. A golden mist formed. The men stood in awe and watched a hazy figure take shape. Slowly, the silhouette refined, until the astral body of the first President, Masonic brother and founding father of the United States, George Washington, formed.

Part of their training as an order was the knowledge of astral travel, reincarnation, and the awareness that time and space did not exist as we know it. These men didn't merely believe, they *knew* that Washington had travelled to them in order to give his blessing to the mission, and to confirm that Laboulaye's instructions were correct. General Washington was after all, a fellow Mason, closely connected, and in fact related to some of its members. His tall, commanding figure remained for several minutes, acknowledging each man present, with hand on heart and a bow, until with a lightning flash and loud boom he was gone. In his place remained ectoplasm, with something swimming in its soupy matter.

Bartholdi approached the substance tentatively. He picked it up and wiped it with his robe, revealing a purple and white beaded belt. He instantly recognized the belt from his art history studies as being made from wampum.

"These are handmade beads made from shells that the natives of North East America used for ornamentation and trade. The first colonists in Washington's day used these beads as their currency with the natives, and each other. They offered their goods in exchange for the beads. The belts were especially valuable, their design had spiritual and cultural significance, and when worn by a native, the belt showed their status within the tribe," he informed the men. He studied its design further. "This belonged to a spiritual woman," Bartholdi said. "The white and purple shells represent the light and dark, the sun and moon, male and female." He shook his head. "The colonists soon realized their worth and found a way to mass produce them, eventually devaluing them as currency. The island of Manhattan was purchased with them, one of the first of many injustices committed by the white man."

Bartholdi's chest felt heavy, and the weight of deep sorrow and regret weighed on his heart. "Our beloved brother, Washington, who incorporates the consciousness of national integrity, has travelled through time, to this room, to make amends." Bartholdi whispered. "Labour to keep alive in your breast that little spark of celestial fire, called conscience."

"What was that? We can't hear you," Henri said.

"Labour to keep alive in your breast that little spark of celestial fire, called conscience," he repeated louder. General Washington had spoken those very words in his lifetime. "When we pass out of this earthly existence, we carry our conscience over with us. Washington has carried this burden all this time, and wants to rectify the wrongdoing. Somehow, we must give these beads back to America, symbolically and energetically, back to the natives. There must be justice for them. Balance must be restored."

Richard Duchene took the beads from Bartholdi's hand and wiped the fluid on his trouser leg. A powerful, unseen force knocked him to the ground, flat on his back and unconscious. The men gathered around, and lay their hands on his body, which shook and jerked about. Another beam of light came through the domed ceiling, and poured straight into Richard's chest, out of his eyes, and up through the top of his head. An otherworldly voice, supernatural in vibrato and tone, whispery, yet forceful, feminine and masculine all at once, came through him. Duchene's breath was so cold it created vapour as he spoke.

"This vehicle which I now inhabit has been given a mission from on high. We stand poised to enter the final phase of the earth's evolution. He has alchemical knowledge, experience, purity, and devotion. He will carry out a most important task." The voice stopped for a moment, and Richard's body lay still. Laboulaye instructed the men to stay in place. His body jerked, inhaled, and spoke again.

"Richard Duchene was known as Aholiab. His task is to esoterically encode the gift that Bartholdi will design for the United States, just as he did when he was known as Aholiab, who along with Bezaleel, built and encoded the Ark of the

Covenant, as instructed by God, through his beloved Moses. This gift is much more than meets the eye; it is much more than a symbol. It will help awaken humanity. When the time is right, Richard Duchene will take on a new earthly form. He will reincarnate in America. Along with his female counterpart, he will fully activate the codes which he will implant in the gift in this lifetime."

Richard's body jerked, and shook again, and a great winged light rose out of him, illuminating the room so brightly, the men had to shield their eyes. Then it was gone.

Laboulaye's hood fell onto his shoulders, as he stared up at the ceiling dome. "We've just seen an angel."

*

Two weeks later, the brothers gathered at the docks to bid Bartholdi farewell on his journey to New York.

"Godspeed!" Laboulaye shouted, as Bartholdi walked up the plank towards the ship. Bartholdi pointed to the anchor hanging off the ship's bow. The brothers all understood what he was saying. The anchor was a Masonic symbol of hope that kept you steady in the storms of life.

Bartholdi boarded the ship, alone and without an exact plan, but his heart was full, and he trusted in the process of the mission. The journey was long and arduous, and each nautical mile tested his faith. He was anxious to get to the New World and make his offering. *Offering of what?* he wondered. He was overwhelmed, yet honoured by the awesome responsibility, but inspiration was not forthcoming. Each day for almost four weeks, he sat on the deck with his sketchpad, pleading with the muses. Each day, nothing came. Anxiety and doubt were taking hold, and his faith waned. On the final day, standing on ship's deck approaching New York Harbour, he had a mystical vision.

She appeared to him.

Bartholdi could hardly breathe as he quickly sketched

Libertas, the Roman Goddess of freedom. He held the paper in front of him, looked at it, and then back at Bedloe Island. *Liberty Enlightening the World.* Her power, and her presence had already existed on the etheric, waiting for the visionary to see her. Bartholdi realized she had been in his consciousness for some time, having designed something similar years ago for the Suez Canal. Although not the right place or right time, the seed had been planted. The Statue of Liberty was born even before he set foot on solid land. *How will I convince them to allow her to be built on that island?* he wondered.

"It is all taken care of from on high," his consciousness answered.

CHAPTER 7

ROSE COHEN
New York
Present Day

Rose allowed her body to sink deeply into the corner of the purple velvet L-shaped couch, relaxing into an oversized cushion; it was her favourite spot, offering the best view of the city. Kombucha tea, ambient music, and a diffuser filled with calming and uplifting oils of bergamot, wild orange, lavender and rosemary, helped her restore a sense of positivity and balance. It was her first time back in the apartment she shared with Adam, before the affair.

She was excited yet apprehensive about the evening's gathering at Edith's, and was trying to keep her nerves at bay. It seemed like a good opportunity to test out some basic Emotional Freedom Techniques she had learned in a one-day workshop in the village. Tapping through feelings was a tool to get to the root of things, and, with any luck, move through emotional responses without getting stuck. With her index and middle finger, she tapped at a spot on her forehead, allowing any thoughts and feelings to come to the surface. As instructed, she voiced them out loud.

"I'm afraid to meet Ananda," Rose said, while tapping away on the top of her head. "I don't know why, but I am."
Tap. Tap. Tap.
And breathe.

Rose changed her tapping to another meridian on her eyebrows. "I'm afraid he will see the truth." Tap, tap, tap. *The truth?*

"That I'm really dark." Tap, tap, tap." *Where did that come from?* She changed position again, this time tapping the sides of her eyes.

"I am dark." Tap, tap, tap. "I am dark." Tap, tap, tap.

Rose couldn't move beyond that thought for about three minutes, repeating the words over and over, until she felt a well of tears rise up. She continued to voice the sentiment, though shakily. It was as if she was facing a repressed truth, admitting that she wasn't all sweetness and light. Tap, tap, tap. She moved the tapping to just under her eyes. "I am dark. I am dark. I am dark. I am dark." Each repeat, and each tap, seemed to make the statement more real, until she collapsed on floor, whining like a petulant child. "Why?!" she cried. "What have I done? Oh, God it hurts. It hurts so much." She curled into a foetal position, and cried until there were no tears left. "I'm sorry. I'm so sorry." *What am I sorry for?*

"I'm sorry," she said, beginning to tap again under her nose. "I'm so sorry. So, so sorry." Rose stayed with that feeling for a while. "I'm sorry it didn't work out between us. I loved you so much." *Did I really?* "I thought I loved you." Tap, tap, tap. "But the truth is, I don't even love myself."

There it was, the core issue. After all those workshops, all the books, the lectures, the readings, all the meditating, the health regimes, the yoga...*still* no self-love.

She picked up her tea, and settled back into the sofa, emotionally exhausted. *Don't take life too seriously. None of us gets out alive.* She giggled tiredly at the message on the mug that was a Hanukah gift from her Dad. *Laughter IS the best medicine. Thanks, Dad.* The intercom buzzed just as she was about to pick up the phone to double check that he still planned on going with her to Edith's that evening. *Who could that be?* She got up and crossed the room to the little black box on the wall.

"Who is it?" she asked.

"Package for you, Mrs Wolfe."

"Thanks. I'll be down for it in a while."

"It's all right. I'll send it up."

Within moments, the bell rang. A small brown cardboard box was left on the doormat. Adam's unruly handwriting screamed from the label. *What now?* She took a deep breath and went back to the couch, held the package for a while, bracing herself for whatever it might contain. She held it to her ear and shook it gently. Something heavy rolled around. She opened it slowly. There was a note. "Found it in the side pocket of a suitcase. I remember how frantic you were when it was lost. Adam."

Rose gently lifted out the amethyst crystal egg she'd bought from an old woman at a street market during a trip to Sao Paulo. The egg had stood out amongst the other second hand ornaments, almost as much as the woman selling it. She had dark wavy hair peppered with wiry greys, deeply lined olive skin, and the most striking, knowing green eyes that Rose had ever seen.

"It's very special," the woman had said. "It's from the deepest part of Brazil."

"It's beautiful."

"It has been with me for over thirty years. Today, I sense it is time for it to move on to its next home."

The colour, quality, and purity were exceptional. It was towards the end of the day, and Rose looked in her wallet to see what was left…roughly twenty-five dollars. She was unsure if she was even in the right ballpark. The woman's eyes met hers.

"Take it. It's not for me to sell."

"Really? Are you serious?" Rose asked, unaccustomed to being given anything, especially from a complete stranger.

"I am sure, dear soul," she said, kissing Rose's hand. "Crystals find you, you don't find them."

It seemed like yesterday, and for a split second, she felt warmth towards Adam for his thoughtfulness.

"Bastard," she mumbled under her breath, with a hint of affection. She held onto the gemstone egg, connecting with its energy, and the energy of the woman who gave it to her. There was such love in her, such gentleness.

Rose got up from the sofa, and carefully placed the egg on a tiny blue Chinese silk pillow, on the white marble mantelpiece, next to a gold statue of Ganesh. The phone rang. It was her father.

"Hi, honey. What time shall I pick you up?"

"You're really coming?"

"Yeah, of course. And the Yankees are playing, so I hope it's worth it. Be ready. Six o'clock sharp!"

*

"What do you wear to an evening with a swami?" Rose wondered out loud, rummaging through her closet. *'Swami', now there's a word you don't use often.*

She wanted to strike that perfect balance of effortless grace and casual elegance. She wanted, no, *needed* to look beautiful, despite her lack of self-esteem. There was a lot of expectation surrounding the evening's encounter.

She settled on a smart, but casual, lilac Indian-style pant suit, with a shawl she'd bought last year to wear to a talk downtown given by a New Age western guru. She recalled the evening clearly. She had paid over two hundred dollars to attend a workshop on manifesting happiness and abundance. But it was clear that the only people getting rich were the ones running it. Over the years, she'd seen so much corruption in the alternative lifestyle movement, just as one might in any big industry. She'd had enough of it. Yes, there were a lot of good, conscious people doing great work, but sadly, in her experience, they were not always the ones putting themselves out there. They lacked the ego and ambition. Rose resolved never to waste her time or money again. *When the student is ready, the teacher will appear*, she thought. She hoped tonight would be better.

*

"The Cohen's are here," Thomas informed Edith over the intercom.

"That's the first time I've been called by my maiden name in years," Rose said to her dad.

They were grateful to have been invited early before the other guests, in order to have a private introduction. There was a noticeable silence in the elevator. Noticeable, because it was rare for the two of them to be lost for words in each other's company. Rose's nerves were getting to her, and her breathing was becoming shallow as she watched the numbers on the elevator rise. The bell rang, and the elevator came to an abrupt stop at the penthouse. As the doors slid open, Rose was relieved to see Edith there with open arms. The older lady pulled the two of them into her bosom, squeezing out some of the anxiety in Rose's body. Her home was immaculate as usual. Rose had never seen it untidy.

"What's that smell?" Samuel asked.

"It's called incense, Dad."

"Ananda brought it with him to bless the room," Edith said, releasing them both and ushering them into the living room. "Can you sense it, Samuel?"

"Yeah, well, I suppose I can. It does feel nice in here. Is there sandalwood in that? Some rose maybe? A hint of patchouli?"

"That perfumery course in Grasse was worth every penny!" Rose added, patting her father on the back.

Richard walked into the room and immediately caught Rose's eye. She held his gaze for a few seconds then quickly shifted her focus on Edith. It had been a long time since Rose had noticed another man. It took her off guard *and* put her on guard.

Why didn't Edith mention how handsome he was?

"Richard, these are my oldest and dearest friends in the world," Edith said. "Samuel and his daughter, Rose."

Richard extended his hand to Samuel. "Pleasure to meet you."

"Likewise."

Rose discretely wiped her sweaty palm against her trouser leg, and took Richard's strong, but gentle hand. Her face was frozen into a false smile. *Be normal!* "Hi. Rose."

"Pleasure."

"I'm sure I've told you about him before, Rose," Edith said, detecting a spark of energy in the air.

"Yes, you have. You met at the ashram right?" she turned to Richard, looking up his tall frame to meet his eyes again. *Holy moly, they're gorgeous.*

"Yes. We did. Several years ago."

"Have *we* met before?" Rose blurted out. Everything about his presence was oddly familiar. If she had been blind, and he was standing near, she would be able to recognise his energy. Rose was totally thrown by the unexpected feelings. She shifted and looked down at her feet, feeling foolish for saying something so trite, but the words had just flown out.

"No, I don't believe so, Rose. Namaste," he said, with a bow. "Nice to meet you."

Edith exited the room to check on Ananda, and Samuel excused himself to the bathroom, leaving the two of them on their own.

"So, how does it feel to be back in the good ol' USA?"

"It's fine," he answered, looking past her, leaving little room to carry the conversation further.

"So you met Edith at the ashram?"

"Yes, that's right," he said with a half-smile, his attention elsewhere. "And you asked that already," he winked. "Will you excuse me a moment?"

She felt foolish just standing there, abandoned and

uncomfortable in her own skin. She regretted coming. She wasn't ready, and there was nowhere to hide. She suddenly felt self-conscious in her outfit as well. She looked the part, but wasn't living it.

After what seemed like an eternity, Richard returned with two cups of chai.

"Thanks," Rose said, taking the steaming cup from him. They sat down on the floral sofa, a respectful distance between them.

Rose watched him closely. She liked the way he held his cup with two hands while lifting it to his mouth, his bronzed skin contrasted against the white cotton shirt. He was the picture of health and well-being. *That's years on an ashram for you.*

She took a sip of her tea. "This is unbelievable. Wow. The flavours are so delicately balanced. What is it? Clove, cinnamon…" Her body was as stiff as their conversation.

"And cardamom, coriander, and ginger," he added. "We brought the spices with us. They grow in Kerala. Oh, and the sweetener. Jaggery."

The awkwardness hung about them like a mantle. *Please make this end.*

"You went to USC, but you're from the bay area, did I get that right?" Rose asked, clarifying something Edith had said earlier.

"Yes, that's right."

"What was your major?"

"Business and economics. I hate looking back on those days, but I guess it was all part of the journey that brought me here."

"Why do you hate it?"

"I don't know. I was such a different person then. Different values I guess."

"Youth."

"I suppose so. But a lot of my friends from those days haven't changed much. My ex thinks I've lost it, no doubt.

What about you? Did you go to college?"

"Me? A Jewish American Princess? Of course I did. But only so I could meet a husband!" she said, only half seriously.

"Oh. You're married!" Richard's relief was palpable. "I met my ex in college as well."

"Oh. No. I'm not anymore," Rose said. "Long story."

"How many people are you expecting?" Rose asked Edith who'd returned just in time to break the tension.

"It's a small group. About fourteen?" She did some quick calculations on her fingers. "Or a bit more. Some close friends, and others from my meditation group. You'll know most of them, save for a few. I'm going to see if Ananda is ready now."

Rose's mouth went dry, her feet and hands went tingly and her heart raced. To her relief, her father arrived back in the room and sat next to her. She took his hand, and they both watched the hallway for Ananda's grand entrance. Everything went silent. No more hustling and bustling from Edith, no chitchat. When she first caught sight of the esteemed guru, she took a deep breath, and her heart thudded. She squeezed her father's hand. Ananda was wondrously dressed in a white floor-length kaftan, and was barefoot with a string of mala beads around his neck. Light emanated from his eyes and burned through her soul in one luminous glimpse. His smile was captivating. She had never before experienced a presence like his.

He walked over and took Rose's hand between his palms. "Truly delighted to meet you, kind Rose. Edith has spoken much about you."

Samuel reached out his hand "Hello, Mr Ananda. I'm Samuel Cohen."

"Samuel wouldn't normally come to an event like this. We're honoured he's put his bridge club to the side for an evening!" Edith joked.

"It was the Yankee game actually."

"Dad!"

Ananda smiled. "I am truly honoured."

Rose studied Ananda's eyes as he talked to Edith and her father. They held such warmth, love, and light. So much light that she felt that if she took his gaze directly, she might not be able to sustain it. He glanced at her fleetingly again, as if he'd heard her thoughts. She felt a warm glow and a vibration in her body. She turned her attention away from him, and looked around the room. Her eyes were drawn to a painting she'd seen many times but never paid much attention to. Dark and heavy, it was a depiction of Moses carrying the Ten Commandments. Moses was painted with two glowing horns coming out of his head, almost like devil's horns. To Rose, the horns looked like they were actually emanating light into the room. The effulgence was extending out of the painting itself. "Do you see that?" she asked her father.

"See what, darling?"

"The picture. Oh, never mind."

The vision stopped as quickly as it came. Rose wondered if she'd just had a mystical experience. "Edith. Tell me about that picture."

"It was given to my father. It's an original print by Moritz Daniel Oppenheim, one of the first widely celebrated Jewish artists."

Edith's father had been an admired lawyer with tremendous integrity and respect for justice. He was also a philanthropist and patron of the arts, often supporting the careers of unknown and emerging artists. Through his contact with them he became an expert on symbolism in art. The painting was left to Edith in his will.

"What does it say to you?" Samuel asked his daughter, curiously.

"I don't know really. I'm just intrigued by the horns."

"Yes, they do look like horns," her father replied.

"Rays of light, from communing with God face to face,"

Ananda said, contemplating the picture as if in altered state. "The hand of the artist was surely guided. In fact, there are two chakras there. The light emanating from them is divine light, a very different quality than regular light. It is imbued with spirit," he said, snapping back into the present.

"I've been taught there are only seven chakras," Rose said.

"There are seven major chakras. People have known about and worked with them for thousands of years. There are others, and two are on the side of the forehead. Once the crown chakra opens, these two chakras activate," Ananda tapped his fingers near his temples. "They are about bringing that divine consciousness back into the earth's vibration. Why do you think they're called temples?" He laughed. "Those two lights that look like horns on Moses, are symbolic of Moses bringing God's wisdom back into the earth's vibration to serve the needs of the people." He paused. "At the time."

"What do you mean 'at the time'? Aren't the Ten Commandments the highest teachings ever received from God?" Edith asked.

"Moses's teaching of the one God, and the rules for living in a moral society, were the highest teachings of that time. They were absolutely right then, when people were fighting and killing each other over whose God was best, and worshipping things like money and success before God."

"Doesn't sound so different from today," Samuel commented.

"Moses was a realised soul, but the world wasn't ready for *all* that was revealed to him. He had to filter it. Humanity was working on the lower chakras – their immediate needs for survival, safety, and supply. And yes, Samuel, that's not so different from today. Those teachings, once integrated, prepared humanity for the next phases of spiritual principles. These next phases came later through other teachers, such as Gautama the Buddha, and Jesus. As people became more receptive, in India, the teachings of Ramakrishna, Ramana Maharshi, and others, elaborated on earlier teachings of Vedanta. Moses's teachings were a stepping stone, or a *tablet,*" Ananda said looking directly at Richard as he emphasized the word. "Teaching us how to live as better humans in preparation for our spiritual evolution and development that would come later. Every teaching, and every teacher, is interconnected."

Ananda continued. "The lineage in certain religions is very strong. Jesus lived and died Jewish. He was called Christ after his death because he had attained Christ consciousness. Christ comes from the Greek *Chrystos,* derived from the Vedic *Krsta* or Krishna, meaning the supreme personality of the Godhead."

"Why are they all men? Did women not attain that same level of spiritual awareness?" Rose asked.

"Absolutely they did. Men have traditionally been in the forefront, while women were kept down, due to cultural and, later, more sinister reasons. There have always been as many enlightened women on the planet. There are several female masters living today, some unknown, and some very well known. One dear sister has incarnated near to me in Kerala. In the past, there was the 'Holy Mother', the wife of Ramakrishna, and of course Mary Magdalene. She was not only the wife of Jesus, but was closest to him in spiritual realisation. During that age, they were the perfect balance of male and female. Of course, as the Roman Church took hold, the divine feminine was driven underground, accepted only by the few, as it is today. Mary was written out of 'his-story', and out of history. She has been written out of consciousness. Those times are changing."

"Thank you for clarifying," Rose said.

"The mistake Jesus' followers made after his death, was to set up the teacher, not the teachings, as the most important thing. This has been the same mistake in all religions, including my own lineage. Great teachers come for one reason only, to bring love and to live the teaching by example. The only thing that separates them from everyone else is their realisation of that truth. Jesus was a Jew. He was a Rabbi, but it was never about religion, or Jesus the man, it was about the teaching he introduced and lived by. There is a time for sitting at the foot of the teacher, and there is a time for standing on your own two feet. In the words of Christ himself, 'If I go not away the comforter will not come.'" Ananda paused. "Samuel, you look perplexed."

"Is it necessary to have a teacher?" Samuel asked.

"A teacher is helpful until you know your own true nature as an unlimited being of light, one with everything. Not just mental knowledge of this oneness, but total awareness. A teacher is a helpful conduit in the same way that a switch is a medium to turn on the light to dispel darkness in a room. Electricity is a wonderful invention, but unless one of us can make contact with the light switch, we remain in total darkness. Light is ever present, ever waiting for us to make the contact."

A hundred thoughts and questions were running through Rose's mind. She had a library of spiritual books, which she had read over and over, and she had attended numerous workshops, lectures, and retreats. But it was in that moment, that finally her soul had been deeply touched.

Edith was beaming. Before she could stop herself, Rose asked Ananda. "Are you the switch?"

"When the student is ready, the teacher appears," Ananda answered softly.

His words hit Rose like an arrow straight through her heart.

"Welcome home," Ananda's eyes spoke to her. She knew in that moment, that her life would never ever be the same again.

"But didn't you just say that people idolise the teacher, not the teaching?" Samuel questioned.

"Perfect, Samuel. Great observation. This is where so

much confusion stems from. A true teacher doesn't seek self-glorification – they only present the teaching. It's up to the student to incorporate it," Ananda looked over at Edith and Rose. "The greatest gift you can give any teacher is for them to be unnecessary in your life. That will be proof that realisation has taken place within. Then people below your consciousness will be drawn to you. This sets in motion a continual evolution and the earth and its people are lifted into greater freedom."

Richard looked uneasy when Ananda mentioned that a point would arrive when the teacher would become unnecessary. There was a flicker of sadness in Ananda's eyes when he looked across at him.

"How do you know that what the teacher is saying is true? Why should I believe what you are saying? No disrespect, but how does one differentiate a fake spiritual teacher, from a real one?" Samuel asked.

"That, my friend, is the age old lesson of discernment, one of the first and most important spiritual lessons, and not an easy one if I may add. Ultimately, this is a principle everyone must acquire for themselves, through self-inquiry, observation, and experiences in this life and other lifetimes."

Rose couldn't believe her ears.

"There is a way to differentiate a true teacher from a false teacher. The true teacher has the ability to change lives for the better, on a spiritual, emotional and physical level."

Samuel and Rose looked at Edith. She was the embodiment of that very principal.

"There are many spiritual teachers in many different religions. There are also teachers whose main interest is to keep you affiliated with them or their organisation. These teachers or teachings may give a temporary lift, or an emotional boost from time to time, which on the surface may look like a healing, but a month or two later, people are usually back where they were. However, remember they are learning the great lesson of discernment, so all is perfect.

When the time is right, and lessons learned, they will find the true path to freedom. Above all, pray for guidance and then trust your intuition."

"Thank you," said Samuel. He looked at the picture of Moses above the mantle again. "I think I'm starting to understand, but I'm having a bit of a conflict. The Ten Commandments tell us not to worship false idols, to look to the one formless God. Yet, here we are, all of us, hoping to get something from you, whether we admit it or not. Well, perhaps with the exception of me, it's too late for me to begin a new spiritual path!" Samuel's words lifted the mood, and they all laughed.

"I am a wayshower in this physical earth vibration, not an idol. I have my own connections, which have their own connections, which have *their* own connections, until we are back to the source, which we know as God. All is one. I am yourself a moment from now. That's all I am. We are all moving up on different rungs of the ladder."

"Now please excuse me. I must spend a few minutes in meditation before the gathering…empty out and prepare for any information that will come through. I am often surprised myself by what happens when we clear the way!"

CHAPTER 8

SWAMI ANANDA DAS
The Statue of Liberty, New York
(Earlier that day)

Ananda was in a state of heightened perception as he climbed the stairs. He sensed Edith worrying about time and the preparations for the evening ahead, and felt Richard's fear of being in an enclosed space. He took a candy from his pocket, and passed it back to Richard in full awareness of the energy it carried from his blessing.

His two companions silently trailed behind him, up the stairs and around the pedestal's observation deck. "Stop," an inner voice commanded. Ananda was rooted to the spot, and unaware of anything around him, when the teaching and vision began.

The voice continued, "This statue is an outer manifestation of an inner temple that was established at the beginning of earth's time. Earth has seven power points, or chakras, and is a macrocosm of the human body. You are now standing on the crown chakra. This space is multi-dimensional and working on many levels," the voice explained.

Ananda recalled his experience in the meditation hut, preparing him for this final initiation. He was in a state of total trust as his attachment to the physical lessened, and he readied himself for the information. His inner eye opened and displayed a moving esoteric montage of the evolution of the spot where Liberty Island existed in the present. It started long before any land was visible. Ananda perceived a golden light streaming down from the heavens into the water. 'As above, so below,' he heard. Then a small land mass arose out of the sea. Time passed, and tides drenched the flat. An indigenous tribe wandered on the plains. He sensed them to be gentle people, connected to the earth.

A Native American woman came slowly into focus. She slid her kayak onto the island. Ananda was in awe of her luminous beauty, both within and without. Ebony braids fell to her waist, and wise dark eyes shone like glistening oyster shells in the sun. She wore moccasins, a cloth dress tied with a purple and white beaded wampum belt, an animal skin draped around her shoulders for warmth, and a golden band around her head. Oysters carpeted the tidal plains surrounding her. Closing her eyes, she emitting ancient, guttural, almost animal-like sacred sounds that carried across the horizon, across time. Her crown chakra glowed. The spirits of her ancestors gathered, and illuminated the oysters which were ready to move on. They guided her to take only what was necessary to feed her people. "Keep the sacred balance of the colony," the ancestors advised.

After filling her satchel, she stood tall, arms and face raised towards the sky. A bolt of vibrant purple lightning came down from the heavens and went through the tip of her finger. Another green bolt rose up from the earth through the soles of her feet.

A human conduit.

Both colours met at the top of her head, and rays of light like a halo spread across the land. "*Paravati.*"

The veils of time were pierced, and he and the woman were not limited by time and space. "I am Gela, of the Lenape Nation. My name means 'keeper of happiness'. My people call this land Lawantpe, or 'crown of the head'." She looked down for a moment, "This country has fallen from its spiritual destiny. Its return to freedom will begin with you. *This* is your final initiation."

In the most unlikely of places, in the greatest capitalist country in the world, surrounded by tourists, Ananda had received information that would change the course of history.

"Ananda," Gela whispered. "I am the guardian of this space. You have heeded the call, opened the doorway, and now many will follow in your footsteps. This spot is beginning its highest level of activation now. Mother Earth's crown chakra is here. She holds a connection to every other power place or chakra on earth. Lawantpe."

Gela physically moved into Ananda's energy field. She took his hand and led him deeper into a vision. Standing in the middle of the beam that went through the Statue of Liberty's body, he was shown seven spinning discs of coloured light ascending from Liberty's base, to the top of her head, the crown chakra. From each disc, rays spread across seas, plains, and mountains, culminating in different countries across the globe. It was clear the earth herself was in an ascension process.

Ananda's consciousness fragmented, then travelled at speed, culminating at each chakra centre. Vibrant colours swirled and spiralled around him at each spot, then shot off back to the Statue of Liberty, passing through his physical body, and then through Gela behind him and into pure, blinding white light. In the next moment, he felt his being expand and encompass everything. Ananda was in everything, and everything was in Ananda.

"There are three earth chakras that you will work with. Three key centres for the spiritual harmonising of the planet as it goes through its final phase of evolution, preparing to move into higher dimensions, where the frequency is faster, and darkness will be dispelled. The three chakras are the base chakra in Jerusalem, the heart chakra in Glastonbury, and the crown chakra here in New York City. Here, now, within you and I, heaven and earth meet upon this spot, to activate and open the door."

She put her hand on Ananda's shoulder. Immediately they were hovering over a city, obscured by a dark, murky cloud.

"Jerusalem. That cloud is a manifestation of all the cries of the people," Gela said. "Much karma will be worked out here, in the base chakra, where there is a battle between spirit and matter playing itself out in war over territory and resources. There is also its opposite – pure religious devotion and prayer. Harmony is close now that the crown chakra is being fully activated. When a chakra is activated by a great soul, the potential for higher spiritual revelation, or its opposite, conflict, will be accentuated in that area. This land is the birthplace of the Christ Jesus, the great soul that came to earth to fulfil his spiritual destiny. In your lifetime, the tides will turn, and physical and spiritual harmony will prevail."

Gela squeezed his shoulder tighter, and a pinhole of light appeared in the grey cloud. It grew wider and wider, until Ananda could see inside a house below. Four men took their places at a table. Although the only light came from a single candle, and from the stars, the house glowed from the outside and from within.

"Divine Light," she said. "They are advanced souls occupying high positions. A Rabbi, Imam, Priest, and Buddhist Monk. All have mastered their sacred texts. All have lived by them to the letter, and advised others on their contents. They are also advanced spiritual initiates, able to reach and embody the higher teachings of their sacred texts, past the literal, and into the mystical. God has brought them together."

"What are they doing?" Ananda asked.

"Each has been visited by a holy one, and been given a task. They have had to step away from their own religion, from their position as religious leader, and embrace each other's faith, becoming a member of their society, attending study groups, ceremonies, and public events. Each embodied the realization that it wasn't about *their* religion. By surrendering their own belief system, and converting to another, they discovered they were all the same. Tonight the four have come back together, having successfully completed their initiation. A gateway to a whole new consciousness has been created."

Ananda witnessed the men's hands come together at the centre of the table, and then rise up, as if one. Exalted, and full of affection, they embraced. The room radiated love, like a flowing river returning to its source. A host of angels gathered, and the four stepped out into the night.

Ananda felt a gentle energy come towards him. Through the veil two figures appeared, a man and woman dressed in white robes, wearing gold and silver headbands. They held hands. Each placed a hand on either side of Ananda's head. "Blessings be upon you," they said together.

"Ananda, my beloved, receive this blessing from Jesus and Mary. You also have overcome the obstacles of life, the tests and the trials."

A burning fiery heat ran through him, followed by a river of peace.

"We are almost complete," Gela continued. "Before you return to your physical body within the Statue of Liberty, your final connection with your light body will be in the green pastures and rolling hills of southwest England, the heart chakra, imbued with unconditional love."

Like an elastic band, Ananda's awareness was pulled towards the United Kingdom.

"A place that I once visited during my initiations while incarnate. Avalon awaits you," the voice of Jesus whispered from the distance.

Ananda's consciousness arrived in the ancient land of Glastonbury, the Isle of Avalon, holy land of the Chalice, within the sacred grounds of the Abbey.

"Pilgrims have been drawn here for thousands of years. It

was established in the beginning as earth's heart chakra, to balance and heal the masculine and feminine chambers of the heart, individually and universally. Here in the Abbey the masculine and feminine meet as one."

All-encompassing love filled his being, as Gela's hands pressed on his shoulders once again.

"You have proven that there is no longer the potential for you to use your power for personal gain. You are ready. Our connection is now at the highest. I am forever with you. We are one."

Gela disappeared into a radiant ball of sunlight. Ananda's consciousness returned to the present. He was now a fully enlightened ascended master, operating within the earth's vibration.

CHAPTER 9

Edith had been thoughtful and deliberate when she chose her guests. The prerequisite was they had to have shown a personal interest in Ananda, or that they had an open curiosity and perhaps even an inner search. Many were going through some sort of personal struggle as well.

And then there was Roger. Edith hadn't intended for him to attend, but she had invited her dear friend Mandy, and Roger was her brother, visiting from Los Angeles. Edith could tell that Roger thought that the whole scene was 'a little flaky'. He was the polar opposite to Mandy and her alternative lifestyle.

The air was thick with anticipation as everyone found their place and settled in. As hostess, Edith had pride of place on a folding chair to the side, and slightly behind Ananda. For her personally, it was a big event.

Some of the guests were acquaintances of Rose that she knew from travelling in the same social circles. Many of them were also regulars at Maison.

Jim and his wife, Katherine, sat cross-legged with their eyes shut, getting into the zone. Sarah and Estelle, known as 'the twins' had smiles from ear to ear, as they scooted closer to the front, near Ananda's chair, hoping to get the best view, *and* the biggest blessings.

A hush came over the room. Ananda followed the path lined with tea lights and flowers that Edith and Richard had prepared earlier. He stopped half way, and Edith scurried over and touched his feet. She then had the honour of circling a flame around him, while Richard rang a bell and chanted a prayer. Ananda once again proceeded along the path through the small group to his chair. Richard followed closely behind.

Edith waited for Ananda to be seated, and then addressed her guests. "I can't believe the day has arrived," she said. "Thank you all for coming this evening, for this blessed opportunity to meditate, and receive darshan from Swami Ananda Das. I know a few of you have already heard my story, but I would like to share it with you all tonight. I will try to be brief." Edith looked towards Ananda.

"Years ago, I lost my husband of over twenty years to suicide. He took his life after an investment with an associate, a friend of ours, went wrong. I never got over the shock, nor did my beautiful daughter, who also took her own life. It was the darkest period of my life. I blamed myself for not coping after his death, for not being there for my daughter. I closed myself off in order to go on. In truth, if I'd had the nerve, I would have killed myself as well."

Edith paused for a moment, and took a deep, cleansing breath.

"After a year or so, with the help of good friends, I took stock and counted my blessings," she glanced over at Samuel. "It wasn't easy. I decided that getting far away for a while would be a good idea. I booked a package tour to India in honour of my daughter who'd always wanted to go. On that tour, I met a woman who'd heard about a teacher with incredible healing abilities, so we took a detour, and travelled for a couple of days to meet him. When I arrived, he took my hand and told me things even my own family hadn't known. The healing of the losses, and the beginning of a new journey began on that day. I've been back to his ashram in India several times since then. Every time I saw him, I invited him to America, but my offer was always declined. 'When the time is right', he'd always say. I guess the time is right now."

With hand on heart, Edith bowed her head.

"Before we begin tonight, I'd like to tell you a bit about Ananda." Edith paused again as the enormity of having Ananda in her house finally hit her. Hands shaking, she picked up the piece of paper from the coffee table and smoothed out the creases.

"I'm going to read you part of an article that Ananda wrote about his own life."

Clearing her throat, she began. "I was born in southern India into a wealthy Hindu Brahman family, and was to study law abroad, in England, when a motorbike accident at twenty-two changed my life forever. No one thought I would live. I recall hovering over my body, attached to machines and tubes, feeling a huge sense of relief, unencumbered by the heaviness of the physical, yet, aware I had a 'self' separate from my body. Next to my bed, my uncle had placed a picture of his own teacher, a great Indian sage, which I was staring at when I heard a voice. 'It is not your time. You must return.' I felt resistant. I didn't want to return. Then as if on a movie screen, I watched my soul's journey, life after life at great speed. Some were noteworthy, others ordinary, and some weren't so nice. I was held and guided through the process with unconditional love. My last two lives were deeply devotional, dedicated to the search for God, at the foot of that very sage from the picture. I then received numerous teachings from the inner plane teachers, given through visions and telepathic communications. In that moment, I knew I must return to this world, and I felt my being snap back into my body. I opened my eyes, and understood that life was about to change forever."

You could have heard a pin drop in the room. Edith put the article down and continued to speak.

"Within days of leaving hospital, people were drawn to him. He healed the sick, and comforted the needy. Word spread rapidly in that part of southern India, and then people started to arrive from the West. The ashram grew up around the needs of the people who came. Until now, he has never left India. Ladies and gentlemen, it is my pleasure to welcome Swami Ananda."

Ananda greeted each person with his eyes. He was welcomed with enthusiastic clapping.

"Good evening, all. It's lovely to be here in this auspicious place, amongst you people, not one of whom is here by chance."

"Well, I am," Roger spoke up. Mandy looked mortified.

"Oh no, you are not, my friend," Ananda answered, and without missing a beat, continued.

"I've known for over twenty years that one day I would come to New York, but I didn't know when. I had to wait for instruction, which I received a couple of weeks ago, in meditation. Things have unfolded rapidly since my arrival. I am very grateful to Edith for her hospitality, and for inviting you all here tonight. Before we begin, let's have a few minutes' silence and let the thoughts and cares of the world slip away. When we do start to commune, you'll find that any questions you have for me will come from a deeper place." Ananda closed his eyes.

The silence was deafening.

Roger cleared his throat, and shuffled in his seat, clearly unnerved by the lack of external conversation. He closed his eyes like everyone else, and after some time became still, until a high pitched bell rang.

"Please slowly bring your awareness back into the room," said Ananda softly.

Edith glanced at the clock on the wall. An hour had passed.

Roger followed her gaze to the clock. "No way. I can't believe it. What the heck? I must have fallen asleep."

"It felt like just a few minutes!" Estelle said.

"That can't be right," Rose added, turning to Edith.

Sarah, one of the twins, raised her hand. "What just happened? We all experienced time passing so quickly."

"Silence is a great teacher," Ananda said. "The key to the doorway of perception. In that space, there is no time. I'm sure some of you in this room have had deep meditations before, and if you haven't you will, as your spiritual journey unfolds. You have just transcended time and space. When we turn within, we aim to transcend those senses and open a doorway to the soul, that intuitive, holistic part of our inner being."

Ananda looked at Roger. Roger was looking straight at him, his arms folded across his chest.

"Thank you," Sarah said. "Oh, and could you please explain to me what darshan is?"

"Of course, Sarah. Darshan, put simply, is being in the presence or having a glimpse of a deity, or a great master or guru, someone who knows his, or her, own divinity, and can therefore recognise and awaken it in you also. That for which you seek, you already are. It is a great blessing to be in the presence of someone who has a God realisation. Edith has invited you here for darshan. I will not make claims about myself, but, of course, Edith is a very intelligent woman!"

As soon as the laughter died down, Roger jumped in with his questions.

"What is God realisation? What has this holy person or *thing* realised? Can you *prove* the existence of God to me? I think God was invented to keep us away from developing our intellect, so the masses can be controlled by the few."

"I'm so sorry about my brother," Mandy said, nudging him with her elbow.

"Pleased don't be," Ananda replied. "I am delighted with your brother's questions. God realisation means to be taken to a level of understanding that is beyond the mind, beyond what you see, hear, taste, touch and smell. You just had an experience of time passing quickly, not from a place of intellect, but from a place of 'knowing' that there is another world beyond these confines. What do you do for a living, Roger?"

"I'm a teacher of economics."

"Wonderful. So students come to you for your knowledge, and I would say you are a very knowledgeable person."

"Hey, flattery is not going to get me on your side," Roger quipped.

"If a student came to you, and said that two times two is five, and they believed it, would you not feel duty bound to enlighten them to the truth that two times two is four? So that their pocketbooks and bookkeeping wouldn't suffer?"

"Obviously."

"And once they grasped the truth their pocketbooks and bookkeeping would come back into harmony."

"Yes, but what are you getting at?"

"The governing principle of mathematics never had an awareness of your student's mistaken belief, right?"

"Right."

"Or when they finally got it?"

"I guess."

"They misunderstood how to calculate. Am I correct?"

"Yes."

"And their accounts suffered."

"Ok, but again, what are you getting at?"

"It is the very same with God, or the creative force, whatever you want to call it. We have separated ourselves from the truth through ignorance. We have miscalculated. Some organisations would prefer to keep us in that ignorance. They are the ones who want to control the masses. There are others like myself, teachers of spiritual, metaphysical and esoteric principles, who help to bring students back into harmonious alignment with the truth, so that your lives don't need to suffer, and you are free. But remember, God, truth, higher self, creative principle, it doesn't matter what you call it, has no awareness of our lapse, or when we make the return journey. There is no judgement."

"I think I may be starting to get it," Roger said tentatively.

"We are all parts of the one, and we are multifaceted, different players on the world stage. Right now, you are the questioning intellect and doubting part within all of us, and Edith is the surrendered and devotional part, which is embracing her journey back towards self-realisation. We all start with doubt, move through devotion, and finally surrender. Most people will only start to move from doubt and seek higher understanding when they've gone through pain, either by losing a loved one, money, position, or a health scare."

Ananda focused on Roger's eyes. "The toughest times are blessings in disguise."

Roger shifted in his seat again, looking uncomfortable.

Ananda continued. "In the moment of questioning, you create frequencies that attract the answer. Whether you accept the teachings given here are irrelevant, you have been exposed to other possibilities and ways of thought. Of course, you have free will to do what you wish with the information." Ananda looked around the room. "Any other questions?"

There was a long silence. Rose felt prompted to ask a question, but didn't know exactly what about. Ananda looked at her knowingly.

"You want to ask me something?"

Rose took a deep breath. "There are people who have really hurt me. I've had a lot therapy, and I've done a lot of work on forgiveness, but I can't seem to forgive them. The hurt still eats into me. Can you help?"

Ananda closed his eyes for a moment.

"From a human standpoint and from a place of ego, it's

nearly impossible to forgive a terrible wrong doing, but when you are on a path of spirituality, you need to inquire more deeply. Why was that person in your life? Find understanding within your higher self, as if you are emotionally detached from the situation, and are viewing it from a higher place. People and events come into your life through the laws of karma and reincarnation, and the law of cause and effect. It is a soul's calling to know itself. When you really allow that understanding to take root within you, you will accept that people and their actions are gifts, angels in disguise, bringing opportunities."

"The opportunity to wallow in self-pity," Rose said wryly.

"Or to gain a few pounds," Katherine said, looking at her husband.

"My friends, they give us a chance to go back and heal old patterns of anger, jealousy, betrayal, power and rejection. There are hundreds of these universal themes played out repeatedly, individually, all across the world stage. Until we truly resolve them, there can be no peace."

"How? How do we resolve them?" asked Rose.

"As I said, move into higher understanding. Allow for the possibility that maybe in a past life you set this situation in motion. Maybe you have previously been the perpetrator of the very issue you are dealing with now, and by forgiving them, you are really forgiving your past self. Now you are putting into expression spiritual understanding, and you are mastering the laws of karma and reincarnation, which exist in three-dimensional reality. Find compassion, Rose. Your paths have met before. After you have exhausted all possible emotions, there comes a moment when the desire to become free of the struggle prevails. Forgiveness is a spiritual law, and you are being asked to put it into practice."

"How can a compassionate God allow all this suffering?" Roger asked gruffly.

Jim chimed in. "Yeah, that's a question that's been

bothering me for a long time. If God is a loving, compassionate God, why is there so much evil?"

Ananda smiled. "Good questions. In fact, they may hold a key to your freedom. What you observe as pain, suffering, conflict and disaster is only ever taking place in the world of duality and separation. It's never taking place in the world of the creator. The creator's world is harmonious, perfect and whole. *We* have built, and continue to build this world, which reflects our state of consciousness. We have created our own world of separation, duality, conflict, and disease. This world we perceive is not God's world, it is the mind's world, Maya, where the laws of karma are played out."

"Wait a minute," Roger said. "Am I correct in saying that karmic experiences are tools and tests to bring us back into truth? If so, this is what I don't get. What is this 'two worlds' business? One of separation and duality and one of harmony? We are in the here and now, in this world. Where is this other world you are talking about? Is it physical like this one?"

"When we transcend duality, and go beyond the five senses, we are living in perfect harmony. It is just as real as the world you inhabit now. In fact, it is the world you inhabit now, but you perceive it differently. Meditation is the key that gets you there."

Ananda asked Rose to come over to him. He took her hand and turned it over. He traced his finger across her palm. "You see this line that curves around your thumb? That's your lifeline. It is long and deep," he said, smiling. "And this line turning just there? That's a destiny line, and those two others that branch out? Where they cross depicts a destined and karmic event that occurred, agreed upon before this incarnation, to bring you back onto the right path. It was never going to be an easy lesson because it is on the karma line of cause and effect, but it returns back to your destiny line further down. That's where you are now. It is all in the higher plan."

"How do I let go?" Rose pleaded.

"Accept that these people were meant to come into your life, that you chose these experiences, not just intellectually, but in your heart. Accept that truth. That's when you can truly forgive, and even thank them at some point. They played their part in bringing you in line with your destiny, and to this room tonight. You are back on your destiny line. The karma has been paid."

Edith noticed Rose and Richard look at each other, and then quickly look away. Edith stood. "I'm aware that it's getting late. Does anyone else have any questions before we conclude the evening?"

Katherine and Samuel raised their hands.

"Okay, first Katherine, and then Samuel," Edith instructed.

"First, I want to personally thank you for coming here tonight."

"You are most welcome, Katherine."

"A lot of people I know, including myself, struggle with depression. Many of us have tried alternative methods to deal with it, and some take medication, but neither seems to really work. What is causing this epidemic of depression, and is there a lasting cure?"

"There is no quick fix for depression. It is a process, and people tend to want to feel better rather than get to the root cause by doing the work necessary for spiritual growth. There can be situations where medication is absolutely right and necessary, but often, depression is a symptom of a soul not listening to its call to awaken. We've all come to the world to fulfil a spiritual destiny, and it's very easy to get side-tracked in this world of duality. Your soul will put pressure on you to stay in line with your destiny. If you don't listen, your body will manifest illness: mental, physical, or emotional. Depression is a call for change in lifestyle, job, relationship, home, personal or familial pattern, or a call to look deeply at some aspect of the psyche that is not in your highest interest. I will say it over and over. Meditate.

Meditate. Meditate. If people can learn to take a few minutes each day to be still, to make a connection with the higher self, the process of deep healing can begin." Ananda paused.

"Meditation allows you to let go of ego identification, and be observant of the changes that need to be made within. If we are continually meeting an issue in the world, and are trying to fix it in the world externally, the fix will not last. The issue is a reflection of something we need to look at within. Through the process of meditation the warrior aspect within you is brought to the fore and the issue is resolved. It is then that harmony begins to be established. For example, if you are consistently meeting anger, rage, or frustration in the world, don't take it personally, but take it as a sign to go within. Look at your own suppressed anger, rage or frustration that needs to come to the light to be healed." Ananda paused again to allow everyone to take in his words.

"Our karmic patterns are tied to our two lower chakras, and the patterns need to be cleared in this life in order for them to be transcended, so the energy can be taken to the higher chakras, which are tied to our spiritual destiny. In meditation you are going beyond the mind and opening a door to awareness. Through meditation, depression will slowly be replaced by a sense of purpose, harmony, and peace. A lasting peace, not a transitory peace. If you are on medication, ask your doctor if you can reduce the dosage little by little, and replace it with meditation each day. A little exercise and fresh air never hurt anybody either! Above all, take time out in nature. It is free medication, the side effects are nil, and the benefits are guaranteed!"

"Thank you," Katherine said.

Ananda looked over at Samuel.

"Why did you finally come to the States now, and what did you think about our iconic symbol, the Statue of Liberty?" Samuel asked.

"Samuel. In my meditation last week, the statue called me to America. And today, while stood in the crown, it revealed many of its secrets. In time they will be shared."

"Now I'm curious," Samuel said.

"Nothing wrong with a little curiosity, but divine timing is at hand."

An emphatic round of applause ensued.

"I wish you the best on your journey," Ananda said, addressing the entire room. "And thank you all for coming. I look forward to seeing you all in the future, in whatever disguise!"

CHAPTER 10

ROSE COHEN
Edith's House, New York City
After the Darshan

"Would you mind staying for a while longer?" Ananda asked as the other guests were leaving. Samuel glanced at his watch, and looked at Rose. It was getting late.

"Of course. We would be honoured," Rose replied, giving her father no choice but to follow Ananda to join Richard at the dining table.

Edith placed a box of 2nd Avenue Deli pastries on the table. "Manhattan's finest."

"My favourite!" squealed Rose, diving into the assortment. She held a black and white iced cookie in the air. "I haven't had one of these in years!" She noticed a flicker of sadness in her father's eyes as she bit into it.

"I've a shop filled with the finest epicurean delights, but it's these things, the simple things from my culture and past, that carry so much more than flavour. Don't get me wrong, you can't beat a good cheese danish, but these also have a story, our story. Yes, what a treat, Edith, and reminder. Thank you." Samuel also took a pastry from the box.

Ananda, delighted by their excitement, picked up a cookie covered in multi-coloured sprinkles. "We've fed our souls, now let us feed our bodies!"

"Amen," Richard laughed, raising his prune pastry in a

mock toast.

"I've asked you to stay because I have something important to share. Samuel, you asked earlier about the Statue of Liberty."

"Yes."

"Each of you has a destiny linked with the statue."

There was a prolonged silence, which was finally broken by Samuel. "My father got the idea for our shop while visiting the statue. He took me there more than a few times when I was a boy. And Rose," he beamed, looking over at his daughter. "She was conceived the night after Elizabeth and I visited the statue together for the first time."

"Dad!" Rose blushed.

"What? It's true."

Ananda continued, "Liberty is the crown chakra of mother earth."

"What does that mean?" Samuel interrupted, completely baffled.

"The crown chakra is the fastest spinning chakra in the human body. The earth has its own chakra system. The Statue of Liberty, and just as significantly, the physical spot she occupies, is the earth's crown chakra. Lady Liberty is a living goddess of freedom, not a dead space of dense copper and iron. She is an awakened embodiment of the divine feminine, pulsating with spiritual life force, and the power to bless and help enlighten those who come to her."

No one said a word, took a bite of food, or even moved. It was too much to take in, too much for them to comprehend.

"Where exactly do we fit into this picture?" Richard asked, breaking the extended silence.

"She has waited for the cycles of evolution that would prepare humanity for the return journey to freedom. The time is now. This planet is dangerously out of balance. The masculine principle has almost completely suppressed the feminine, and caused separation from that which is sacred.

We are heading towards unthinkable disaster."

Rose set down her half-eaten cookie, noticing that only the chocolate half remained. *How fitting.*

"The Statue has always been a point of power for the few, but it is now being activated for the many. Humanity can destroy itself by failing to heed her call, remaining in the lower karmic struggles of power, greed and selfishness. Or, we can continue the journey upwards towards the higher chakras, integrate the sacred balance of the masculine *and* feminine, the principles of creativity, compassion, empathy, oneness, union, and connection to nature." He paused. "True freedom and wholeness will prevail. It is a question of when, not if, it will happen. The outcome very much depends on a combination of things falling into place." Ananda turned his attention to Richard, and then Rose. "The total activation of the crown chakra at the Statue of Liberty depends on you."

Me? Rose felt suspended in another reality, almost outside of time. She couldn't even look at Richard. *Why me?*

"Liberty will be a place of pilgrimage, like the holy cities of Mecca, Jerusalem, and the Vatican. Even now, before its full activation, people are being touched when they visit. Artists have been inspired to create, business people have been guided to further opportunities, and healers have received greater abilities. She is now ready to work at the highest vibration, but her full potential isn't fully activated yet, in the three dimensional sense."

"That's a lot to swallow," Edith quipped, chewing on a metaphorical *and* physical mouthful.

"Edith, your purpose was to bring me here, us here," Ananda said, looking over at Richard. "To the statue, to your home, and to make contact with Rose. There is more to it, but now is not the time."

"Where do I fit in? What do you want me to do?" asked Rose.

"Rose," Ananda said, taking her hand. "And Richard," he said, taking Richard's hand also. "In this life it is your destiny to open the doors to her full activation so that others can walk through them."

Rose allowed herself a quick glance in Richard's direction. Ananda's words confirmed the connection she already felt, but didn't want to face. After all, she wasn't ready to go there with any man, and he certainly didn't look interested. *He's a monk, Rose. Get a grip.*

"First, you both must go through the ascension process yourselves, and integrate the balance of the masculine and feminine within. Then the masses can follow in your footsteps. Your journey will culminate at the crown chakra back here in New York City."

Rose didn't feel like someone who would have such a grand destiny, and she certainly didn't have a clue how to even begin. She wasn't even sure what he was talking about.

"How?" she asked.

"It involves an inner and outer journey."

"A journey?"

"Has there been a desire over the last few months to understand your family history, your ancestors?"

Her eyes widened, and she felt a mixture of wonder and fear. "Ananda, just today I was looking at pictures of my mother's family. I don't know that side very well. Yes, I do have the desire to understand my ancestors, very much so. I felt this so strongly, literally just today."

"You and Richard both carry a memory, something in your DNA, that is tied to the higher unfolding of the crown chakra. I am sending you on a mission. You can choose to go, or not. Nothing is good or bad. If you agree then the first part of your journey is to heal and open your heart chakras. It is about whom you will meet, the places you visit, and how they will touch you. Some of these places carry a very high energy conducive to your journey of spiritual awakening. This journey will ultimately signal the next step for many others who are coming up the ladder behind you. So what do you say?"

"My heart says yes, my head says no," Rose replied, beginning her tapping ritual on her hand under the table, as her breathing became shallow. "I mean you haven't even said what the journey is!"

"That is your head talking, my dear. Your heart knows. Yes or no?"

Rose shut her eyes, and asked her heart to reveal its truth. "My heart says to trust. So I guess I'm in!"

Ananda turned to Richard.

"With all due respect, what *exactly* is the journey?"

"You will not come back to India with me. You will accompany Rose to the heart chakra of the planet. Glastonbury, in the United Kingdom."

"Glastonbury!" Rose was delighted. She had always wanted to visit Glastonbury. She had read the *Mists of Avalon*, and had a friend who had visited some years back. Said it was a place like no other.

"I'm not going back with you?" Richard asked, looking embarrassed by the audible shake in his voice.

"No, Richard. The world calls."

"But I've spent years renouncing the world. Letting go of my ego attachments and desires, my yearning to be something, somebody. I became a monk. Why must I return to the world now?" He hung his head. "I'm sorry for asking. I do trust you."

"If you remain with me, you will never find yourself, Richard. This part of your journey must be taken without me. I am always with you. Remember, it is the teachings, not the teacher."

"My head says yes, my heart says no," Richard offered solemnly.

"Well, then, it is done. Richard's head says yes, Rose's heart says yes. That is just as it should be, a perfect balance of analytical and intuitive already! Congratulations. I bow to you both. Let your grail quest begin!"

CHAPTER 11

ROSE COHEN & RICHARD DUNNE
Newark Airport, New York
Present day

"Ladies and Gentlemen, this is your captain speaking. My name is Captain Bill Brown, and my co-pilot is Captain Tom Mathers. It is our pleasure to welcome you on this beautiful Boeing 787 Dreamliner from Newark to London Heathrow. The flight time is just under seven hours. We will try and make the trip as comfortable as possible for you."

Richard gripped the armrests tensely as the plane taxied down the runway, increasing its power and speed, until its nose lifted, and it rocketed upwards towards the heavens. A thud from shifting cargo startled him, and he grabbed onto the seat in front.

Rose relaxed back into her seat, leaned over and watched as the city of her heart disappeared underneath the clouds. She'd been to Europe a couple of times before, once with her parents to Paris, and another time with Adam to Italy. Both were great trips, but she had to admit that she was always happy to return home. She wondered why it had taken her so long to visit the UK, especially considering her great-grandfather was British.

She recalled the last moments with Ananda, when she, Richard and Edith had taken him to Newark for his flight back to India. Just before walking through the security gates,

Ananda had embraced Edith warmly, thanking her for her care and hospitality, then kissed the palms of Rose's hands, and then Richard's, before bringing them together. It was an awkward moment, and a very powerful one at the same time. She had absolutely no idea what Richard was thinking about it, or her. What did he feel, if anything? Richard gave nothing away. It made her question her own feelings. Were they just fantasy? She was determined not to let her feelings be known, but men always had a sixth sense for those kind of things, or maybe she was just more obvious than she thought.

"I look forward to seeing you all again," Ananda had said as he turned to go through customs. Rose had sensed that Richard took reassurance in Ananda's last words to them, and her heart had softened. She felt for him more than for herself. She knew it was hard for him to leave the ashram and the close physical connection he had with Ananda.

*

The seatbelt signs finally went off. Richard reclined his seat, settled back, and went over the last week's events in his mind. He thought about Edith, and how much he had enjoyed his time in her home. She was caring, warm and genuine. He thought of the hours they'd spent at Maison with Rose and her family. He envied the close bond that existed between them all. He'd enjoyed their open and loving conversations, and the way they'd expressed their feelings towards each other. He felt as though he'd grown in their company, and had become more open himself.

This was not a typical Dunne quality. His own family just weren't very expressive people. Words were used sparingly. Richard's grandfather attributed their disposition to the Irish Potato Famine gene. Not much time for emotion or sentiment when they were busy trying to survive. His great-grandparents, the Dunne's from County Wicklow, had left Ireland during the famine and settled in Boston. Great

Grandpa Sean quickly built a successful contracting business which employed people to work on the railways spreading across America. 'To work is to achieve' was his motto. This Dunne ethos was handed down the line. Richard's grandfather had eighty people working for him, and was a pillar of Boston society. Then Richard's father had left the family business after falling in love with a girl from San Francisco. He moved west, where he set up a prosperous accountancy firm. The Dunne men were driven for success in the material world, though it was something that Richard struggled with. He had got caught up in it himself to begin with, but as time passed, he had lost interest in acquiring more money and more things.

The plane shuddered, and the seatbelt sign came back on again. A baby screamed from behind, startling him out of his thoughts. He turned and watched the mother pacify her child by putting her finger in its mouth, which seemed to do the trick. Richard turned back around in his seat, and fumbled to insert his earphones. He quickly searched for a station to take his mind off the turbulence. Led Zeppelin's classic anthem 'Stairway to Heaven' immediately brought him back to his painful and lonely teenage years.

Richard had followed in his father's footsteps. He embraced his studies at USC with vigour, took advantage of his opportunities and family contacts, and built a thriving import/export business through the San Francisco and Oakland ports. The price he paid for his dedication to his business was his own marriage.

Richard considered his marriage to his college sweetheart to be his greatest failure. The only blessing was that there were no children involved. After the split, Richard's biggest shift occurred when he went on a retreat at the Krishnamurti Centre in Ojai. While there, he met a man who'd just returned from India. He told Richard he should go, said the trip would change his life.

The rest was history. Albeit history in motion, if he had

understood Ananda correctly. Richard thought he'd renounced the world, and yet, he now felt deeper in it than ever. Every step had led him to where he currently sat: on his way to the United Kingdom on the next stage of his spiritual path, feeling, quite frankly, very confused, and somewhat resentful of Rose.

*

A good-looking young man, with slightly orange skin and a hint of eyeliner, tapped Rose on the shoulder. "Anything to drink?" His fluorescent smile was startling.

Drinking wine on a flight always made Rose feel ill. Jack Daniels and Coke was a firm favourite, but the caffeine would keep her up. "Gin and tonic, please."

"Ooh, very colonial choice," he said playfully.

"You have a beautiful accent," Rose said. England was becoming more real by the moment.

"Orange juice for me."

"You don't drink?" Rose asked before she could stop herself.

"I used to enjoy red wine. In fact, my mother invested in a winery in the Sonoma Valley, which is now incredibly popular. Proved to be a good gamble for her. But anyway, I haven't drunk alcohol since I went to India." He held his cup of orange juice up to her glass. "Cheers, Rose."

"Cheers to you, Richard. Tell me, why do you think that Ananda has sent you with me?"

"I don't question Ananda's reasons."

"Oh. Sorry." His curt response had made her feel silly for asking. She withdrew into herself, and after dinner and another drink, found she could no longer keep her eyes open.

*

Richard silently chanted his mantra. Ananda had told him

that whenever he chanted it, they would be instantly connected. Running his fingers around his mala beads under the blanket, he recalled one of Ananda's great teachings. "Whatever is sacred to you, is secret. Do not wear your spirituality. Carry it within you." Ananda had never set himself apart as separate or different. Richard lived by this, and it had served him well in many situations, including in the ashram and his travels in India, and certainly in the west.

When he opened his eyes, Rose's eyes were closed. Her head gently rested on a travel pillow, and her silky brunette hair was flowing softly down her shoulder. She looked vulnerable, but also beautifully feminine in a pink and green satin flower dress that had slid up above her knee, revealing the shapely curve of a toned thigh. Richard carefully reached under her seat for a blanket, unwrapped it, and gently placed it over her shoulders and lap. A small smile crossed her face, and a very soft 'thank you' passed her lips. His hand brushed against hers, and he shivered. The energy between them was palpable.

In his youth, he'd had many flings and relationships. While he was married he'd also had a few dalliances, of which he was not proud. But since going to India, Richard had taken a vow of celibacy and hadn't been in a relationship for four years. Ananda had not placed it upon him; it was a personal choice he'd made when he gave himself over to a spiritual life. Beautiful women of all nationalities visited and lived at the ashram, many whom he'd connected with and escorted as one of Ananda's main hosts and organisers for Westerners. He kept in touch with a few, mostly via email. He'd felt a particularly strong soul connection to Sinead, the Irish woman he'd met when he first arrived at the ashram, and the two of them corresponded quite frequently. They even phoned each other on occasion. He had called her from New York to tell her he was coming to Glastonbury. Sinead was delighted.

"I may just have to come see you!" she'd shouted.

"Dublin is only an hour's flight away. I've always wanted to visit Glastonbury!"

Sitting on the plane now, Richard only just remembered this conversation. He hadn't mentioned it to Rose, but he couldn't imagine that she'd mind, or indeed that Sinead would actually come anyway. *Rose.* For the first time in a long while, he felt attracted to a woman in more than a platonic way, and it didn't sit well. *It is a test.*

The flight went quickly, and before they knew it, a meal box with orange juice, a muffin, and a breakfast burrito was served. The captain announced it would be only forty-five minutes until landing.

"I know this landscape," Rose whispered, as the plane's wings cut through the clouds and the lush green fields framed with hedgerows came into view.

*

Rose's relief was palpable when she spotted her Louis Vuitton monogrammed bag finally pop onto the conveyer belt. Richard heaved it onto the cart alongside his well-travelled rucksack. "What do you have in this thing? It weighs a ton!"

"Thing? That 'thing' cost an arm and a leg."

"Yeah, of a poor, helpless calf."

"I'll have you know that this bag is made of canvas."

"Whatever. It's still a waste of money. And pretty ugly."

"Didn't they teach you non-judgement in your spiritual studies?"

"Touché."

As they came through customs, somewhat bedraggled and more than a little irritated with each other, Richard spotted a kind-looking elderly gentleman holding a board. 'Richard and Rose Dunne' was scrawled across it in thick black ink.

"Hey, you think that's us?" he said, elbowing Rose.

Rose raised an eyebrow when she saw it. "In your dreams." *What am I, thirteen?*

"Hi. I'm Rose *Cohen*," she said, when they reached the man holding the sign. "This is Richard *Dunne*. I think you may be our driver."

"Are you going to Glastonbury?" the man asked.

"Yes, with a stop at Stonehenge on the way?" Richard said, wanting to be sure.

"Well then, yes, I am your driver. I'm Nigel. Sorry about the error. How was your flight?"

"Great," Richard said.

"Did you get any rest?"

"Not much. But this lady did. Snored like a trooper."

"I did not!"

Nigel took their cart, and they made their way towards the parking area. "Did you know the original runways here at Heathrow were laid out in the shape of a six pointed star?"

"You're kidding!" Rose elbowed Richard and rolled her eyes.

"It's true. I just saw a program on the BBC about it last night. Did you know that a hexagram was often referred to as the Seal of Solomon? Wonder what it all means. And now you're going to Stonehenge! God help you."

*

"Do me a favour, Nigel," Richard asked, grasping the handle inside the door as they pulled out of Heathrow and onto the motorway.

"What's that?"

"Drive on the right side of the road?"

"Ha! The amount of times I've heard that from you Yanks. So what brings you folks here?"

"We're coming to trace my family history. My great-grandfather came from Somerset. But that's about all we have to go on." Rose really had no idea what they were doing, bar some cryptic words from Ananda. Richard didn't either. Truth be told, the ancestor thing was really the only concrete bit of their story they could hold onto, and definitely the only thing they could say to people without seeming totally mad.

"Call me old fashioned," Nigel said, looking at them both in the mirror. "But why have you kept your maiden name?"

"Oh, uh, we're not married, I mean we aren't even..." Rose stumbled over her words. "We're friends," she finally managed to say.

"Oh, I beg your pardon. Sorry, I..."

"No pardon necessary," Richard said. It's a compliment to be paired with such a gorgeous lady. I'm her, um, guardian."

"Her knight," Nigel added.

"And I'm wearing spiritual armour,' Richard whispered in her ear.

His voice, and warm breath in her ear were electrifying. *What's this sudden change of attitude?*

"What?!" Rose covered her eyes with one hand and pointed towards a sign up the road.

"What?" Richard asked, fearing a driving emergency. He read the sign out loud. "'Cats Eyes Removed.' What the heck?"

Nigel laughed. "Don't worry, they're just road markings. Reflectors."

"Phew! I thought I was entering a scene from *The Wicker Man*," Rose said, uncovering her eyes.

"Well, paganism *is* alive and well in Britain, Ms Cohen. But as far as I know, no one removes the eyes of cats."

The car zoomed over the hill, and down a steep slope. "Look over there," Rose said, as Stonehenge came into view over the horizon.

"The druids and pagans come here in their thousands,

tens of thousands, on the solstices and equinox. When the seasons change from light to the dark and back again. In fact, I believe there's one coming up soon!"

"How about that?" Richard remarked.

Rose sat up to get a better view.

"That's just incredible. It's older than America."

"Way older," Richard said. "The United States is only just over a couple hundred years old. Stonehenge is what, a couple of thousand?"

"Try over five thousand," Nigel corrected.

Rose looked back at Richard. "It's so tiny. Not what I expected at all." She rolled down her window, allowing the warm wind to blow on her face. *The country air smells different, it has a unique quality, as if it carries memories of the soil, the stones, and the pollen, holding the history of ancient times.*

"The visitor's centre is just over there," Nigel gestured as they turned off the road, into the parking lot. "Pick up your tickets there and they'll bus you down to the stones. I'm gonna grab myself a coffee. I'll be waiting here for your return."

Rose and Richard were both quite disappointed when they learned that access was only allowed around the perimeter, not into the circle itself, except by prior arrangement. Nonetheless, they hopped on the shuttle full of anticipation. Rose had done a lot of research into the sacred site. She was determined to feel and experience the energy rather than just listen to the history of the place, so she and Richard switched off their audio guides.

As they both approached the stones, which stood majestically in the open plains, Rose sensed that they were ancient and wise, and had seen many things. The sky was almost an electric blue, and the green grass was vibrant. The air was clear, clean and fresh. Closing her eyes, she tuned in to the energy of the land, and then approached a path around the stones with reverence, hoping to connect with them.

It was almost inconceivable to her that ancient man could have transported them without machinery. The bluestones came all the way from Wales, roughly two-hundred miles away, and the *Sarsen* sandstones from the Marlborough Downs, twenty miles north. She looked across the landscape.

Rose followed the path, which crossed an ancient processional avenue, which lead up to the main entrance to the circle. Richard followed closely behind her. She intuitively closed her eyes again and felt a current of energy run up from the ground, up her legs, into her spine, and right to the top of her head. When she looked down, there was a stream of glowing light leading from her feet heading towards the stone circle. In a flash, it was gone. "Communicate with the ancestors," she heard.

"What do you mean?"

"What do you mean, what do I mean? I didn't say anything," Richard asked, confused.

She realized that the male voice had come from within. She'd heard about clairaudience, but this was her first personal experience with it.

The two walked the periphery, stopped at intervals, and appreciated their sacred time on the ancient landscape. "Imagine the people from long ago. Early man. Their essence is still so present. You can almost imagine witnessing a ceremony."

"Maybe even a sacrifice!" Richard added.

"Hey, look. There's a face in that stone."

"You're right! It's a wise old face. Been around for a long time. Seen many things." Richard knew from his meditations, and time in India, that all things, including dense matter, had a presence, a God substance. The Native Americans called them Stone People, and knew them as the record keepers on Mother Earth, teachers of the history of the planet.

"Yes. Many things. But he's not giving anything away." Rose responded.

"Reminds me of my relatives in New England. Stone faced!" Richard joked.

Back in the car, Rose thought about her clairaudient experience. Had something opened up in her? Had the landscape triggered something, some latent ability? She hoped it wouldn't go away. Who was that voice? One of her guides maybe? She'd always wanted to receive information directly for herself, rather than paying someone for a reading. She felt they often told her what she wanted to hear, not what she needed to hear.

"According to my SatNav, we're just about an hour from Glastonbury, depending on traffic."

After just over seven hours in England, it already felt like they'd been there for months. New York, Ananda and Edith, all felt a lifetime ago. However, in that moment, Rose felt very connected to her mother, and was excited about exploring the land of her kin.

They exited off the main road onto a roundabout, and then a smaller country road. Rose noted every sumptuous detail. The old stone cottages and manor houses, the giant oaks, chestnut and maple trees, the wildflowers, and hanging baskets spilling over with foliage. She observed the climbing clematis, the endless fields and hedgerows, the stone walls, and the rolling hills in the distance. No words could adequately describe the feeling of driving towards Glastonbury. It was as if a holy presence was accompanying them to a holy land.

"That must be the Glastonbury Tor!" Rose exclaimed. The medieval tower was perched at the apex of a ridged green mount dotted with people and sheep. "This is straight out of a fairy tale!"

The road twisted and turned as they approached the Isle of Avalon, but the Tor always appeared high above the horizon, a beacon far and wide.

The mound's velvety green and flowing curves beckoned her. A sudden flash appeared to illuminate the tower like a lighthouse. A second later, the Statue of Liberty appeared in her mind's eye, reminding her once again of the lighthouse from her dream. *This must all mean something.*

"I can't *wait* to walk up there. Richard, remember, I mentioned it? It's known as the gateway to the underworld."

"Ooh, sounds fun."

"I can't believe I'm here. I'm so excited!"

Welcome to Avalon...the legendary land of King Arthur.

The car passed the sign, turned a bend, went down a hill, and through the thriving town's High Street. It was heaving with activity, even so late in the afternoon. Colourful characters meandered along the road in flowing goddess dresses, and hippy chic clothing. Hipsters and tourists drank pints of lager or afternoon tea outside cafés and pubs. A little boy swung a wooden sword, while his barefoot little sister with faerie wings and a face covered in chocolate trailed behind, the parents, unburdened by worry, were strolling a few meters away. Everyone looked happy and relaxed.

"You have reached your final destination," the Satnav informed. They pulled onto the curb in front of a Gothic Medieval building with stained glass windows.

"Here we are, the George and Pilgrim Hotel. You should find everything you need on the High Street."

"If you need crystals, or spells cast!" said a tourist, who happened to be walking by.

"Thanks so much, Nigel, for delivering us safely," Rose said, shaking his hand.

"You are most welcome, my lady. I better get going. This isn't the most practical place to stop."

Nigel set their suitcases on the sidewalk, and with a nod, drove away.

"It's like Haight Ashbury in San Francisco. I feel right at home," Richard said, noticing a sign across the street above an entrance to a courtyard: *The Glastonbury Experience. Imagination, Transformation, Inspiration.* "Except for those gargoyles!" The creatures stared menacingly down at him from the fascia of the hotel.

Rose had found the George and Pilgrim Hotel on Glastonbury's tourist information website, and thought it looked just perfect for them. It was central and full of character. "The George and Pilgrim dates back to the fourteen hundreds," Rose said. "It's the oldest purpose-built pub in the west, made to house pilgrims coming to visit the abbey, according to the website," Rose added.

A thick atmosphere hit them as soon as they entered the building. It felt as if they'd stepped through a portal in time, and where time had left its footprint. Every glorious detail echoed the past.   Stained glass windows, slate flooring, wooden beams, antique marble table with a gilded mirror, candelabras, a tapestry with a scene of a knight and lady on horseback, and a sword hanging on the wall. Every item was a piece of history.

"Hello, fair maiden." Richard hid behind a suit of armour and raised its arm.

"Don't do that!" Rose yelped.

*

Richard felt unsettled and distracted from his true goal of self-realisation. Increasingly, he was finding it difficult to retain his peace outside the ashram, or without Ananda around. His spiritual disciplines and practices, which he had spent the last few years trying to master, were starting to slip away. It was all fading in importance in the face of an enticing, intriguing, and beguiling world. Richard had to remind himself to stay connected, to keep his mind and heart focused on God. He watched as Rose was enchanted by the theatrical décor, and he felt disgusted. He was disgusted by his own judgments and opinions, which were starting to close him down, and separate him from truth. For this, he blamed her. *I'll have to watch that one*, he thought. *Everything I see on the outside is mind created, and a reflection of something I need to look at within myself.* Ananda's words came to him. "Be in the world and not of it. Hold your peace." Of course, it was all a test. Richard acknowledged that he hadn't really learned anything if he couldn't do that. *This is going to be tough*, he thought, fingering the mala beads in his pocket.

CHAPTER 12

ROSE COHEN & RICHARD DUNNE
GLASTONBURY
Present Day

Rose shut the hotel room door, and took a look around. She dropped her bag on the floor and then flopped backwards onto the oak four-poster bed. She ran her arms up and down the jacquard duvet, feeling its luxurious texture, like she was a child making an angel in the snow. The trip had taken its toll, so she drifted happily off to sleep underneath the green velvet canopy with golden fringe and huge puffy tassels on each corner. She was in a deep sleep when she was woken by a knock on the door.

"Are you ready? Rose, are you up?"

She fumbled for her watch. "Has it been forty-five minutes already?" she muttered loud enough so that Richard could hear.

"On the dot," Richard replied.

"I must have fallen asleep. I'll be ready as quick as I can. Meet me downstairs in the pub."

Rose found Richard waiting at a wooden banquet table, with centuries of merrymaking etched into its surface, including a knife jab or two from past confrontations. Flickering shadows danced against the walls from candles in the hearth of a stone fireplace. Rose imagined a buxom wench holding two foaming goblets of ale popping her head over the bar counter. *I've seen way too many movies.* She spotted an old man with an aged face and Dickensian attire, hunched over the counter nursing a pitcher of ale. She nudged Richard.

As if he'd heard her thoughts, the man picked his head up and looked over his shoulder at them, one bulging eye staring, while the other drifted off to the side, lifeless.

"He looks like a pirate," Richard whispered.

The man grinned, uncovering a set of stained, crooked teeth.

"Oh brother, I heard the dentistry here left something to be desired," Richard joked.

"Where's you two from?" the pirate said in a hefty Somerset twang, beckoning them to join him.

"New York," answered Rose. Richard nodded in agreement, not wanting to get into his life story.

With the back of a leathery hand stained with nicotine, he dragged a straggly string of greasy hair from his good eye, and reached out for a handshake. "Alfred Grimsby," a waft of sour breath came out with the words.

Rose took his hand, reluctantly. "Rose, and this is Richard."

"A fine couple ye are, like Arthur and Guinevere thee selves," he said, his good eye changing direction towards an Arthurian tapestry. "Their bones is buried over in that there Abbey."

"Really? No, I didn't know that," Rose replied.

"There are many hidden things laid buried in this land, Ynys Witrin, the Isle of Glass. You can see into other worlds through the veils. I have my own crystal ball," he knocked on his glass eye with a long pointy fingernail.

The barmaid looked apologetically at the two. "It's also known as Avalon, the Isle of Apples. Alfred's family have been cider makers here in Somerset for generations. Strong stuff. Right, Alfred?" her voice turned up a notch.

"That's right, cider, we call it Scrumpy. Give 'em a little

taster, sweet chops," he gestured below the bar.

"You don't want too much of this," the barmaid said, as she poured the cloudy golden liquid from a plastic jug.

"None for me," Richard said. "I don't drink."

Alfred let out a huge guffaw, "Nonsense," he said. "You're not one of these puritanicals they got here, are you? Town's full of 'em. Them hippies is taking over with their carrot and seaweed drinks. Never heard of such a thing. I've never had a day's illness in me life. Scrumpy'll kill anything."

"I'm allergic," Richard said, to avoid a debate.

"What about you, darlin'? Hey. You sure is pretty."

Rose smiled and lifted the glass. "Why not? Cheers."

"To your good health, luverrr'," he replied.

Rose drank it down in one go. "Oh, that's awful!" she shrieked, her mouth puckering up in disgust.

Alfred's body bounced up and down as he laughed heartily. "It'll sure put hair on your chest."

"Thanks. Just what I need." Rose took a sip of Richard's lemonade to try and get rid of the taste.

"We've only got a few days here. Any suggestions?" Richard asked, eyeing the door, ready for an escape route.

"Patience, Richard," Alfred spat.

There it was again, that lesson of patience. He couldn't get away from it, like he couldn't get away from Alfred.

Alfred stared at Richard for a moment, and slugged down the last of his cider, tipping it back to get every drop. He slammed the glass down, and slumped over the bar in an apparent stupor.

"Come on. Let's get out of here," Richard said, pulling Rose by the hand.

Alfred lifted his head from the bar. "If it be yer first time to Glastonbury, go to the old church on the hill first. The old church on the hill," he repeated.

"You mean the Tor?" Rose said.

"It be the gateway to the underworld. The land of Gwynn

ap Nydd. There've been them people who went up, and never came down, and some who came down stranger then they went up. I haven't been up for forty years. Only ever been up once. You'll be ok, pretty lady, now that you've drunk a little of my elixir. Not sure about him though, Mr Goody Two Shoes. Take the old pilgrim path up Bovetown at the top of the High Street. You's pilgrims not tourists. And don't furget to ring the faerie bell at the entrance. You need their permission. Oh, and before you Yanks leave, don't you furget the Abbey across the road there. Bless their holy souls. They had this place built in the 1400s. The very place you're standing in. Housed the pilgrims, and dare I say." He cleared his throat and patted Rose on the bottom, "relieved the monks of their piety. They still haunt this place. Had a drink with one last week at that table behind you!" Alfred laughed and threw his head back in enthusiasm, nearly falling off the stool.

*

A scraggly, barefoot man with dreads and an acoustic guitar sat on a bench outside of St. John's Church, with an even scragglier mutt at his feet. As they walked by, as if on cue, he strummed the instrument, and sang the first verse of 'Bridge Over Troubled Water'. There was a tinge of foreboding in the words. Richard reached into his pocket, and dropped a small handful of change into the man's hat. The dog sniffed it, seemed to approve, then lay back down.

"That was a lot of money!" Rose said.

"Was it? Ah well. Not your concern."

Rose frowned. Was the attitude his normal personality? Or was it reserved exclusively for her? She couldn't figure out which would bother her most.

A small, heavyset woman in a straw hat and a brown tweed coat stretched snuggly around her middle, stood at the top of the High Street at a crossroad with basket of flowers and groceries on her arm.

"Excuse me, are we anywhere near Bovetown?" Rose asked.

The woman looked up from under the rim of her hat, exposing her cornflower blue eyes. "Well isn't that funny? Follow me, dear. I live in the Old Chapel halfway up. Where are you going?"

"We're supposedly following the old pilgrim's route to the Tor."

"What a coincidence. My house is the old pilgrim's rest stop. Travellers used to wash their feet in a stream that runs straight through my living room."

Rose felt comforted by her gentle energy. The woman had an open, trustworthy, apple-shaped face. Like Miss Marple, Rose thought, offering to take the woman's basket.

"Thank you. That's so kind, dear. I'm not as young as I used to be."

"I'll take that," Richard said, taking the basket from Rose. Rose noted how nice it was to have a man around to consider the little things, and wondered if her earlier judgements had been misguided.

"Would you like to come in for a cup of tea and dip your feet before your journey?" the woman asked as she puffed while walking up the steep hill. "If you have time, that is."

*

Richard recalled how the Moslems in India washed their feet as a spiritual cleansing ritual before going to worship in the Mosque. Even in his own youth, they blessed themselves with holy water before entering the Church.

"Yes, let's," he answered, looking over at Rose for confirmation.

He recalled one of Ananda's talks about rituals before prayer. It was an act of humility and surrender, cleansing oneself of the human mind to connect with the divine mind.

Richard had found it difficult when people bowed and placed their heads on the ground in front of Ananda. He couldn't do it for months, until he realised that he was bowing to the God within himself, and in bowing to Ananda, he was surrendering his ego identification and habit of self-preservation. In fact, Ananda always bowed to the audience before he began a talk.

They walked to the cottage up a pebble path, lined with a border of summer's most vibrant, herbaceous lavender. The sunlight bounced off a metal watering can, and bees buzzed around pots of geraniums. A fading wisteria climbed over the front of the stone cottage, and honeysuckle weaved its way over the entrance to the porch, perfuming the warm air.

"My name's Mary," she said, breathlessly, popping her hat on a coatrack draped with canes, umbrellas, and jackets for all weather.

"I'm Rose. It's really kind of you to invite us in. This would never happen in New York!"

Richard extended his hand. "Nice to meet you. I'm Richard."

Mary slipped off her plain black loafers, and leaned against the cold wall to roll off her sagging stockings. They followed her lead and removed their boots and socks as well. Mary then raised her skirt to her knees, and danced lightly around in a shallow stream that trickled slowly across the slate floor, meandering its way across the room, before dribbling down a drain at the opposite end. She then dipped two fingers into a little silver basin on an old wooden crucifix hanging on the wall above, touched her forehead, made the sign of the cross, and gestured for them to follow suit. Richard shrugged his shoulders, took Rose's hand, and led her into the water.

"It's freezing!" Rose shrieked.

"Shhh," Richard whispered, squeezing her palm tightly. "May our journey be guided and blessed."

"Amen," added Mary.

"Amen," said Rose.

"Don't you get cold in the winter? I mean with all the damp?" Richard asked.

"Nonsense. Follow me." Mary led them into the kitchen. "That's an Aga, darling. Keeps everything dry and cosy. It's a cast iron workhorse."

The monstrosity occupied practically an entire wall. A big basket of coal rested nearby.

"It's a heater, a dryer, and cooker in one! Makes the place nice and toasty," Mary said, filling a kettle from the double porcelain sink. She placed it on top of the range and few stray drops sizzled on top of the burner.

"They sure make you ladies tough here," Rose said.

"They don't come any tougher," Mary smiled, winking at Rose.

Over tea they learnt that Mary Macintyre was a spinster from Scotland. She was a retired school teacher who had always wanted to be a nun, and came on pilgrimage to Glastonbury twenty years ago. She saw the cottage for sale, and bought it without a second thought. Mary now spent most of her time being the guardian of the Old Chapel, volunteering at St. Margaret's Hospice charity shop, writing in her journal, consuming copious amounts of tea and biscuits, and occasionally, when guided (as she had been today) she welcomed guests into her home to be blessed by the sacred waters. Mary Macintyre learnt that Americans talked very loudly, and a lot, and that Richard and Rose had only just met a couple of weeks ago, and really didn't know how they ended up there. When they left, she collapsed into her rocking chair, exhausted, and drifted off to sleep, contented that she'd done her service for the day.

*

The two left Mary's delicious company, and huffed and puffed up Bovetown, and on to Bulwark's Lane as instructed.

It was a magical landscape. A handful of spotted black and white dairy cows grazed lazily on green pastures dotted with daisies, buttercups, and purple clovers, while others shaded themselves under giant oaks, or roamed freely in the apple orchard. Robins and finches flitted in and out of the hedgerows, chirping birdsong. Mystery was in the air. Nothing felt ordinary.

As they reached the end of the lane where it met Wellhouse Lane, the Tor came into view. Brilliant sunshine embellished nature's pallet, invigorating the blue sky, green grass, and grey stone. A spritely woman and her cocker spaniel were sprinting up the hill. She pointed towards the top of the road.

"We must look lost," Richard commented.

"Lost souls, more like."

"Rose, I am far from a lost soul. Don't you understand that I've spent the last four years at the feet of a satguru? Do you even know what that means? A satguru is an enlightened saint whose life's purpose is to guide initiates, like me, along the spiritual path, the summation of which is the realisation of the self through realisation of God, who is omnipresent," Richard said with an irritated tone.

"Point taken," Rose replied, feeling stupid.

"Those are kissing gates!" the woman with the spaniel, who was now halfway up the Tor, shouted back at Richard and Rose, as they reached the entrance. "One goes through first, and has to kiss the other to let them in!"

Both Richard and Rose felt their faces flush. After a moment's awkwardness, Richard ventured through, then kissed the back of Rose's hand, and bowed. "Enter, my fair maiden."

Rose looked relieved. "That must be the faerie bell Mr Grimsby was talking about. Let's go try it!"

They gathered a bunch of pebbles and Rose tried in vain to hit the iron bell, which would grant them 'permission' to enter the Tor. "I'm hopeless. You do it for both of us," she pleaded.

"One more try," he said, handing her a heavier stone. Rose focused and closed one eye like she was throwing a dart. "Success!" she spun in a pirouette on the ball of one foot as the bell clung. Richard hit the bell on his first go.

"Show off."

"I have a request," Richard said, as they started their ascent. "Do you think we could go up in silence? I need a bit of contemplation time."

"Sure, no problem," Rose said.

"I've been a man of solitude for a long time, and I've been thrown into the world at the deep end."

"You don't need to explain. We're not married or anything," she choked over her words. "You can do what you like."

Richard sensed anger in her voice, and it irritated him. Women were strange creatures, full of contradictions and demands, and their emotions confused him. He couldn't read them. He'd always got into trouble with Mandy. She'd thought he was aloof, and insensitive to her feelings.

There was another turn-style kissing gate at the entrance to the Tor, but because of the no talking rule, Rose took the lead and walked through it as quickly as possible.

Slowly, they made their way up. Richard thought of the ashram and how much simpler life was there. It had rules, schedules, boundaries, and there was a goal. Unlike now, where he felt like he was spinning out of control with no focus. On the other hand, he was enjoying experiencing new things, and meeting new people. And Rose, well, despite trying his hardest to stay detached, he was growing fond of her. He found it difficult to admit – even to himself – that he was attracted to her. It frightened him. He felt determined not to give it any power, or give his feelings away.

They stopped at a bench halfway up to catch their breath and have a drink of water, and took in their surroundings in silence. Rose tapped Richard and pointed to a bird in the distance that was hovering in one spot in mid-air with a 'How is that possible?' face. Richard pointed to a band of grey clouds drifting their way. Uh-oh, he thought looking at Rose, who noticed them as well.

The path wound around the side of the Tor, opening up to an expansive view of the surrounding countryside.

They only had a short row of steep steps to go, but their thigh muscles burned, and Rose had a painful blister forming on her little toe. "Damn, I should've worn these in before coming," she burst out loud. Richard looked at her.

"Sorry," she shrugged.

"We made it!" Richard blurted, his chest heaving.

"I don't think I could have talked even if I wanted to!" Rose said. "Well, actually, I did want to," she added.

"That was tough," Richard said between gasps. "Didn't think I was that out of shape."

The wind carried a strange hollow noise that sounded like an ancient call from the tower. Through the archway, a young man with blonde dreadlocks blew into a long wooden pipe almost as long as his body. Richard and Rose went over to him.

"It's a didgeridoo," the young man said, wiping his mouth.

A strong gust of wind blew through, and a raven perched itself on a ridge of stone towards the top.

"The raven is a messenger. Especially in Avalon," the young man said, reaching into his pocket. "It's a sign that magic and synchronicity are happening. You'll be at the right place at the right time." He took a small laminated picture from his trouser pocket, and laid it down in his upturned rasta hat that housed a bit of loose change and a handwritten note: 'Donations for my pilgrimage to India'."

Rose and Richard stared at each other in disbelief; the picture looking up at them from the folds of the cap was a picture of Ananda.

Richard's heart quickened. "I hope you make it," he said,

dropping a ten pound note into the hat.

"Thanks, dude! That's ace."

The clouds were moving in closer. Richard put his jacket down to sit on, and patted the ground next to him. "Let's take a few moments before we go."

Rose sat beside him. "My mom said the weather here changes every half hour. We're long overdue for rain...'Get out your brolly,'" Rose said, in her best British accent.

Their eyes met, and in that moment, it was as if Cupid's arrow had struck. The attraction they had both tried to hide was now full blown love. It came out of nowhere, undeniable, unavoidable. Richard was overwhelmed. The feeling surfaced from his depths, and enveloped him. He was captivated by Rose's face, which shone brightly. Her eyes glowed, her smile was radiant, and her voice was like music. Everything about her made him feel alive. It was magnetic, and he longed to pull her close to him. He blinked, and hoped she hadn't noticed, or sensed the change in him.

"What?" Rose asked, almost shyly.

Richard looked at her intensely. "What's going on, Rose? Why are we here? I'm confused. I haven't felt like this in years. I don't know what it is, if it's a past life thing, or a test, or maybe Ananda just sent me to look after you, but I'm feeling something."

She took his hand. "I don't know either," she responded softly, with a hint of longing in her voice.

He looked into Rose's eyes, and it was as if all time had melted into one moment. Her eyes, the gateway to her soul, remained, but the rest of her face changed into a journey of soul recognition through the ages. A faint memory of the many lifetimes they'd shared began to emerge. The fleeting image of Rose's gaze behind the visage of a cavewoman, morphed into the face of a Medieval lady, then a Victorian dowager, and then futuristic humanoid.

Rose wrapped her arms around him. He stiffened, but she held on, until his resistance began to fade, and he felt himself softening into her embrace. Time stood still, and they experienced a oneness that was the truth of their souls. They were suspended in an aura of love. A raven cawed in the distance, and then flew overhead. Richard's phone vibrated in his pocket, breaking the magical moment.

"Who the heck could that be?" he pulled his phone out of his pocket, saw the name on the screen, and walked away from her.

CHAPTER 13

ROSE COHEN & RICHARD DUNNE
Glastonbury
Present Day

Rose was saddened, and a bit surprised by his abrupt departure after their intense connection. She grabbed her coat, ran back into the tower, and sat on the cold stone bench, pulling her coat around her for protection against the wind.

She felt rooted to the spot, determined to be strong and not allow negative thoughts and insecurities to run riot in her mind. This is not abandonment. It's a phone call, she repeated to herself. Her rational mind accepted this, but her emotional body launched into panic attack mode. The suddenness of that distinct 'fight or flight' reaction made her realise that she hadn't had one in a while. Not since the meeting with Ananda, in fact. The rain was getting heavier, and the wind carried it into the tower, determined to soak her from head to toe. She got up and went to join Richard, who had his back turned to her, talking on his phone.

"It's great to hear from you, Sinead."

Rose's heart sank.

"I can't believe it! Yes. I'm on the Tor. Wait, I can't hear you," he said, speaking louder. "I'm on the Tor!" he shouted, louder still. "I said I'm on top of the Tor. Sinead, I'll call you back in a minute." He put the phone back in his pocket, protecting it from the torrential downpour, and grabbed

Rose's arm. "Come on. That was Sinead. From the ashram. She's in Glastonbury!"

"What?" Rose's heart skipped a beat. "Well, that's a coincidence."

"I can't believe it. I let her know that I was coming, but I never thought, well, she said she'd always wanted to visit. Come on. I've got to call her back."

Rose had heard a lot about Sinead, and she knew how fond Richard was of her. Now that she was here, it felt like an intrusion, a threat even. She felt open and vulnerable, and resentful that this stranger had burst into their bubble. This was her journey, their journey. Again, the raven cawed overhead.

"Come on. Hurry up!" Richard shouted over the wind as he dashed down the steep path ahead of her. Rose followed, taking care as the cement path was uneven and slippery, and she'd nearly taken a tumble already. Rose resented him rushing down the slope, resented the noticeable excitement and eagerness in his gait. Ironically, this time, her lips were firmly shut. Even with no vow of silence imposed, she couldn't bring herself to speak, lest she say something she'd regret. All of her words felt stuck in her throat. Probably for the best, she thought. *Rose, get a grip. You are not in a relationship. You have no right to feel possessive.* But she did. The wind whipped wet strands of hair across her face, and she was grateful that they hid her frozen, forced smile. Richard stood at the bottom of the path, waving her to hurry down.

"Are you ok?" he shouted.

"Yeah. Fine," she croaked back.

The storm passed just as quickly as it came, and once again, the sky was a clear vibrant blue.

"Hang on a second," Richard said, wiping his phone screen and putting it to his ear.

"Sinead! You're here? Yes, the George and Pilgrim. Bottom of the High Street. Yeah, of course. When? Okay, see you then. Me too."

He put his phone back in his pocket. "That was Sinead. The one I told you about from the ashram. She's here!"

"Yes, you said that already," Rose replied, with a tinge of annoyance in her voice.

"She's going to meet us tonight for dinner at the restaurant near our hotel."

"Great," Rose said, managing to feign enthusiasm. "I'm really looking forward to meeting her."

*

The first thing that Rose noticed was the bright red curly hair. She knew it was Sinead the second she walked through the door, even before she threw her arms around Richard. She watched as they held each other for what seemed like an inappropriate amount of time.

"Rose! I feel like I know you already!"

Rose took inventory of Sinead's features and measured them against her own attractiveness. No competition. Hands down, Sinead was by far more beautiful. And that accent. Sinead was a real threat. Rose felt awkward and almost oafish next to this faerie-like creature. Suddenly, the strong body that she'd worked so hard to cultivate, seemed masculine, and her tawny features felt, well, dark. If he likes her, he could never find someone like me beautiful. We're so different, Rose thought. Then she chided herself, noting how quickly women tended to size each other up, and worse yet, how critical they were of themselves.

Sinead embraced Rose's slightly stiff body, which quickly softened in the warm embers of Sinead's aura. Rose noted the silkiness of her curls against her cheek. Her perfume with musky, woody, and heavy flowery notes filled her senses like an aphrodisiac. She liked Sinead immediately, which made her feel comfortable, and, oddly enough, uncomfortable at the same time.

"The second I was sure you were coming, I checked for cheap flights from Dublin. There was an offer I couldn't refuse. You know I've always wanted to come here, and you were the perfect excuse. Besides, it's been a long time hasn't it?"

"Too long," Richard answered, which made Rose sit up straight.

"Richard's told me quite a bit about you and your family, Rose. I can't believe Ananda left India." Sinead leaned over the table to make her point to Rose. "Must be for a very special reason," she winked.

"I've heard lots about you as well, Sinead," Rose smiled, warmly, her energy finally settling.

The evening progressed and Rose discovered that she genuinely liked Sinead. The bottle of wine they shared between the two of them didn't hurt things either. At one point she nearly forgot Richard was there, she was so wrapped up in their conversation. A genuine friendship had begun, but there was still the matter of Richard's affections. Rose excused herself to the ladies' room, finally feeling comfortable enough to leave the two on their own without her watchful eye. Besides, she couldn't hold her bladder any longer.

*

"She's terrific," Sinead said when Rose left the table.

"Yes. She is," Richard answered unenthusiastically.

"For God's sake, what's the matter with ya? You looked like someone died when you said that," she fell back into her chair. "Ah ha! I've got it," Sinead exclaimed, putting her forefinger to her lips.

"Got what?"

Sinead smiled playfully, shaking her finger at him, "Now I understand."

"Sinead."

"Her stiff hug, and sizing me up. She likes you." Sinead leaned in, taking Richard's hand in hers. "And you've developed feelings for her."

Rose walked in at that moment and saw the two holding hands.

"How long are you staying for, Sinead?" Rose asked, taking a huge swig from her glass of wine, even before taking her seat.

"Now that was impressive!" Sinead joked, as Rose drained her cup, trying to quell the tension. "I head back tomorrow morning. I literally came in for one day to get a taste of the town, and to see Richard. I've got work on Monday." Sinead turned to Richard. "I've got another teaching job."

"Really? All this way for just one night? What a shame," Rose said, sounding quite insincere.

Sinead looked at Rose, and then at Richard. "It was all meant to be. Perfect timing. I got to see my best friend," she said, emphasizing the word 'friend'. "And meet you, Rose. That's what I came for. I've been here since early this morning. I've done the Abbey, the Chalice Well, and I'm gonna go up the Tor in the morning. I'll be back someday."

"I'm sorry you won't be here longer," Richard said, wiping food from the corner of his mouth. "We're here for less than a week ourselves. I could stay longer. There's so much to see."

An attractive man entered the restaurant with a gold Celtic harp in tow. He sat it down at the end of the restaurant near their table, and greeted the owner, who promptly brought him a bottle of beer. The man played enchanting folk songs from Andalucía to Ireland. It was a beautiful night of sharing, conversation, and laughter. Sinead joined him in singing a version of the Irish folk song 'She Moves Through the Fair'. She sang like an angel as well as looked like one

Richard had never seen Sinead look and feel so beautiful. He was grateful that he had found a true soul friend in her.

She understood him so profoundly – seemed to be able to read his innermost thoughts. He trusted her wisdom and counsel, which he had sought many times in India. And she was right, he had developed feelings for Rose. At the table that night, when he thought about going back to India, he was surprised to find its appeal waning. In the presence of a heart that was beginning to open, anything was possible.

"You must go to the Abbey first thing," Sinead said as they were saying their goodbyes. "Try and get there early when not too many people are around. There's a presence there. Something special. Believe me," she turned to Richard.

Richard held Sinead's face in his hands and studied it like a work of art. He kissed her forehead. "It's been great to see you, Sinead. I hope it's not too long before we meet again."

Sinead pulled Rose aside and whispered in her ear. Rose nodded, and Sinead winked at Richard. "May our paths cross again. God willing."

CHAPTER 14

ROSE COHEN & RICHARD DUNNE
TEMPLECOMBE
Present Day

Templecombe was an expensive twenty mile long taxi ride from Glastonbury. They travelled there to begin an investigation into Rose's maternal ancestral line. Rose felt that her great-grandfather was somehow playing an important part in her journey. She knew it by the way she'd felt compelled to stop at the photograph in her hallway that day. Then Ananda had confirmed everything she had felt.

The church of St. Mary was their first stop, to see if there might be a parish record of the family. Unfortunately, the door was locked when they arrived. As they were leaving, two immaculately dressed elderly people bade them good day. The man, in a tweed blazer and dickie bow tie, steadied himself against his pushbike. The woman had long grey hair tied in a lose bun, and wore a black pleated skirt, cameo broach, crisp white blouse, and diamante spectacles hanging from a chain around her neck. Rose felt distinctly shabby in her tracksuit and sneakers, even though they were designer.

"Do you know when the church opens?" Rose asked.

"Are you American or Canadian?" questioned the man.

"We're American."

"What brings you here to our little village?" asked the woman.

"I'm here to trace my ancestors. I think my great-grandfather came from this area. We don't know much about him. All we have is a picture with Templecombe, Somerset written on the back of it. I have a copy with me."

Rose noticed the two exchange a funny look. She unfolded the picture from her bag. The old woman stared at the photo, and then at her companion. "How much do you know about your great-granddad, dear?" she asked.

"Well, nothing really." A butterfly flitting around the woman distracted Rose momentarily. "There's a lot of mystery around him. My grandfather came to America after the war with only a few pictures, including this one of his father. He never talked much about his family. We all thought it was too painful for him."

"May I?" the woman asked, gently taking the photo from Rose.

"Sure, of course."

She retrieved a magnifying glass attached to a chain in her pocket, and ran it over the picture, drawing it in close, and then holding it away, moving the magnifying glass up and down until it focused at just the right spot over her great-grandfather's lapel. "Yes, it's him," she said to her companion. She looked up at Rose. "We've been waiting for you."

"I'm sorry?" Rose wasn't sure she'd heard correctly.

"I'm Maggie," the woman said. She pointed to a small pin on Rose's great-grandfather's jacket. "Look."

Rose took the magnifying glass, and focused in on the pin of two knights riding a horse.

"I was given guidance in my prayers yesterday to come to the church this morning because there was someone I had to meet. I know it's you because this pin on your great-grandfather's lapel is from the order of the Knights Templar."

"Knights Templar? What? I'm confused. How can that be?" she looked at Richard who shrugged his shoulders, wondering if he'd stepped into an episode of the X-Files.

"Forget chance," Maggie said intensely, looking at Rose. "When you are in the flow, and working with your destiny, you are tapping into grace. Synchronicity. There's more to this village than meets the eye."

"I thought the Knights Templar were from the thirteenth century," Richard interrupted.

"My dear, the order was never disbanded. It simply went underground. Come with me, I've got something to show you."

They walked through an iron gate into the grounds of the church, where several ancient yew trees kept a watchful eye over the tombstones.

I'm Rose by the way, and this is Richard."

"This is Edward. Come, Rose," Maggie called her over to a yew. "Put your hand on its bark. Connect with it and ask for its blessing. It is known as the immortal tree, and its magic is renewal, regeneration, everlasting life, rebirth, transformation and, most important to you, access to the otherworld of our ancestors."

Rose approached the tree and put both her hands on its trunk. At first, she felt silly. She was a city girl through and through, and didn't think of trees as having any presence or power, but she was open, evolving, and nothing of her old self was a given anymore. Rose felt herself transforming, metamorphasising. As she let go of her old beliefs, and breathed into the experience, she could feel the tree's wisdom, it's energy, and, yes, its blessing. She felt almost as if its branches were bending down like arms and were holding her, and grounding her.

"The yews have given their benediction."

Rose looked over at Maggie. Something had definitely happened. Rose gave thanks to the tree, and was drawn to another ancient yew nearby. Sitting on the ground, with her spine up against its trunk, she closed her eyes to meditate for a moment. Within seconds, a vision began: it was of the

Temple of Jerusalem. Rabbis were giving a blessing, the fulfilment of a mitzvah. Then, clear as day, one of the priests turned to face her. The face of her father, Samuel, was looking at her.

"Your patriarchal lineage descends directly from a priest in the Temple of Solomon, my child," Rose heard, from a discarnate voice.

Rose emerged from the vision feeling almost weightless, and slightly disoriented. *Maybe this is what an out-of-body experience feels like*, she thought.

"What happened over there? You look like you've seen a ghost?" Richard asked, concerned.

"I came here to trace my mother's ancestors, but have just been given information about my father's side of the family. It seems all the Cohens are either connected to, or are direct descendants of the original temple in Jerusalem!" She remembered the tallit. *Ah, that's how the story started.*

"Rose, are you serious? That's incredible. And the Knights Templar were the guardians of the temple, and the pilgrims. This is all getting very interesting," Richard said, sounding intrigued.

"Come now. We must be getting on," Edward said. He took them over to an unmarked grave. "Thirteen men are buried here. Their bodies were discovered over in the field, just a short distance away. Nobody knows who they are," he said, looking over at Maggie. "Well, nobody will admit that they know. There is something here that needs protecting."

Maggie turned to Rose, and spoke in a tender voice. "We're pretty certain your great-grandfather is buried here. Along with twelve others, all descendants of the original Poor Knights of the Temple of Solomon, better known as the Knights Templar. They were here guarding a secret, and they paid with their lives."

Rose stared at the mound, with its weeds, and overgrown plants. What a sorry ending. She sat next to the grave with her hands splayed out on the ground, and sent all the love and light she could muster deep into the earth. She made a vow to return some day to clear the site of debris and to plant flowers.

"So that's it then," Rose said to Maggie and Edward. "Do you know anything else about him?"

Maggie took Rose's arm and helped her to her feet, then reached out to take Richard's as well. "Come. I want to show you something."

The four of them left the church grounds, walked along a winding lane, and down a dirt track. Maggie stopped, turned Rose around and pointed to a crumbling farmhouse. "Look familiar?" Maggie asked.

"No, not really."

Maggie held the copy of the photo in front of her.

"Oh my goodness."

"Your great-grandfather lived here. His name was Victor Templier. He was a direct descendant of one of the original nine Templars from France, who founded the order. When your family came to England it was changed to Templer. He was very high up in the order. I know this because he wore his pin on the right side, over the spiritual heart, not the physical, which was the accepted place."

"My great-grandfather was French? How do you know all this, Maggie?"

"My grandfather, and your great grandfather, were part of the same order. I am one of the order's few living female members."

"I didn't know there were women in the order," Richard said, sounding perplexed.

"That's because there weren't any until the 1700s, and even then they were undercover, working silently behind the scenes as teachers, nuns and midwives. It was and will be women who take the wisdom and consciousness out into the world, living it by example. Rose, for the last seven years I have been prepared and have been receiving guidance that everything was being taken care of, right down to being told

- 145 -

to be here today at ten this morning." Maggie took Rose's hand and gently squeezed it. "Such is the beauty of our God. She knows our need before even we do." Once again the butterfly was back circling them both.

"Butterflies are really following us today."

"The butterfly is a symbol of transformation and rebirth. It starts with legs and ends up with wings. You, my dear, are being reborn."

Walking along the narrow road back to the church, Rose stepped back into the hedgerow to let a car pass, and her hand swung straight into a stinging nettle.

"Ow! Something's bit me."

"You've been stung by a nettle. Harmless, but very painful. Don't worry. The antidote is near." Maggie gathered a large dock leaf from the roadside. She rubbed it together in her hands until the green juice came out, and smeared some on Rose's hand. The sting went away instantly. "The remedy for every problem is always close at hand."

Rose felt it was more than just a physical healing. Something in her mind had shifted. She was being balanced.

They arrived back where they'd started, at the church.

Maggie reached into her pocket, took out a large iron skeleton key and dangled it in the air. "I am the doorkeeper of the church."

Richard and Rose looked at each other.

"Of course you are, Maggie," Rose said, smiling broadly.

Maggie inserted the key into the heavy wooden arched door and pushed it open. Richard and Rose entered first. A cool breeze and the distinct smell of damp was a welcome relief from the sticky summer's day. They sat down in the front row on the wooden pew, admiring the vaulted ceiling and stained glass windows.

"Can you feel that?" Richard asked. "There's a presence here, a palpable holy energy, like at the ashram."

"It is very still," Rose agreed.

"There is a reason why you are here today, and why this

village is so important to you." Maggie looked directly into Rose's eyes. "You will receive a lot of information today. Listen carefully, both of you," Maggie said, looking over at Richard. "Our paths will only cross this once, but all will become clear in time."

Rose and Richard were in a state of heightened perception. Every fibre of their beings were hanging on to the words that were to come.

"In the thirteenth century this village was a training ground for the crusaders, and a meeting place where Knights Templar from all over Europe gathered to make important decisions. They assembled on the grounds where your great-grandfather's home currently stands. In 1945, there was a discovery, or to be more precise, a rediscovery, of one of the most important religious icons of the Knights Templar, and of all time."

Rose took a deep breath. Richard put his hand on her knee reassuringly.

"A painting of the head of John the Baptist appeared underneath crumbling plaster in the ceiling of the outhouse at your great-grandfather's house. The woman who bought the place after he was killed discovered it quite by accident."

Rose was riveted. She looked over at Edward, who appeared to be standing guard at the door. "Why is it so special?" Rose asked.

"The Knights Templar revered the head of John the Baptist, even over Jesus. In his day, he was known as the wild-man and vagabond, because he simply could not be controlled by society, or bound by its laws. His unconditioned mind made him an open vessel of divinity, endowing him with the 'freedom of spirit' necessary to initiate Jesus into his Christhood in the river Jordan."

"What does it have to do with us?" Richard asked.

"The painting that was discovered is actually part of a wood panel that formed the door, which stood as a gateway to enter the Knights Templar inner sanctum, here at its headquarters. Before entering, a member had to stop, knock, and say the words 'Here before you I stand and knock. An empty vessel in service to the one'. It represented leaving the human mind behind, and opening the door of perception to the divine mind. The door was an allegory of the door of perception. I'm telling you this, my dear, because I know you are being prepared. The painting carries a powerful energy. The eyes penetrate and follow you, and it moves something within and without. This is the essence of a holy relic. After Herod took the life of John through a beheading, John's disciples took the linen which the head had been wrapped in. It had left an impression much like the Shroud of Turin; it was handed down, and guarded with total secrecy. The Knights Templar have it in their possession. The painting itself carries the energy of his unconditioned mind, and the paint they used was made from a drop of his blood preserved within a piece of beeswax, also taken at the beheading," Maggie paused. "We must leave you alone now, Rose. We will wait outside for you."

Maggie took them over to the wall where the panel was displayed, nonchalantly, with no pomp and ceremony, and no protection – it wasn't even encased in glass. It was just there, perhaps the most holy of holy relics, hidden in plain sight.

Rose sat down and contemplated the enormity of the information she had been given. It was like her life was suddenly a movie script. The story was outrageous, yet felt true. Rose wondered if she was getting swept up in the rantings of two old eccentrics, or whether she had actually met two contemporaries who were really part of the ancient Order of the Knights. She wondered how she would know the truth, and what she would do with the information once she did. Rose approached the panel and knocked on it lightly.

"Here I stand before you and knock. An empty vessel in service to the one." The words flowed out of her, as if rising through her, not from her own mind. She immediately felt overwhelmingly tired. She couldn't keep her eyes open. She closed her eyes and rested on a pew near the painting. She remained in a semi-awake state for several moments until a cloak of sorrow enveloped her. She was grief stricken from a heart-breaking loneliness. It felt like a death. As she surrendered and accepted the feeling, the sweet smell of roses filled the air, and along with it, she felt a presence. A gentle peace filled her being. For a split second, she wondered if she had actually physically died, but could still feel the wooden pew beneath her hand.

"You are now ready. You have come through the death and rebirth," a voice that felt like it was coming from within and outside of her spoke. "Although it has taken years of preparation, activation has now taken place."

Drawing her attention further inwards, she felt a rose bud softly open in the cavity of her chest – its delicate petals unfolding, releasing perfume. An overwhelming love for all creation ensued, which brought with it a steady trickle, followed by a fountain of tears. Tears of joy, tears of sorrow, tears of gratitude, compassion, empathy, and then knowing. A knowing that this was love. This was the essence of the sacred feminine, and that it had to be brought out and awakened in the world to readdress the balance of the masculine active principle with the intuitive receptive, and that she and America were a crucial part of it.

Someone was tapping her on the shoulder. "Rose, are you ok? What happened to you?" A butterfly flew through the front doorway and landed on Rose's hand.

"Richard. I think I've just been reborn."

Rose walked outside, straight up to Maggie, and stood in front of her, practically nose to nose. Maggie retrieved a tissue from her pocket and dabbed her own eyes. The two stood looking at each other for several minutes in deep communion.

"It is done," Maggie said taking out a small antique cotton handkerchief from her handbag, holding it as if it was a most prized jewel. She unfolded it slowly, revealing a tiny wooden carving of a pinecone. "Rose, this has been waiting for you. It was sculpted from the painting, from the back of the panel." Maggie whispered in her ear, "It's made of Acacia wood, from the same tree used to build the Ark of the Covenant. It's been kept safe by the order, waiting until the right time for it to be taken out into the world, when a critical mass was attained. You are to take it with you. Remember, it carries and contains the energy of the mind that cannot be controlled by the external world."

Rose held it in the palm of her hand. It was warm and charged. "I'm honoured. But what am I to do with it?"

"I don't know exactly. You need to take it somewhere. You will know."

Rose instinctively touched it to her forehead and heart, and a picture of the Statue of Liberty appeared in her mind's eye. Chills ran down her body. "I think I know where it's going," she smiled.

"Keep it hidden, always," Maggie instructed.

Rose put the cloth deep in her jacket pocket, thankful it had a zip. She gave Maggie a long embrace.

"We won't meet again. My work is done," and with that, Maggie walked away. Within weeks, she would transcend her body and return home.

CHAPTER 15

RICHARD DUCHENE
Paris/New York
1875

After many meetings, negotiations, and debates, Bartholdi convinced the New York governing bodies that America should accept the gift from France. Laboulaye mailed a formal request for it to be constructed on Bedloe Island. Bartholdi, full of excitement and enthusiasm, returned to Paris, with an agreement that America would fund the foundation for the statue, and the pedestal on which it would stand. France would fund the building and shipping of the statue.

By the efforts of the lodge, one million francs had already been raised to begin the construction, but much more was needed. Laboulaye formed the Franco-American Union in 1875 to rally support. Bartholdi's plaster miniature model of Liberty raised a further six hundred thousand francs from the public. Unfortunately, the deadline of the hundredth anniversary of the Declaration of Independence was missed.

Liberty's head and torch were displayed in the US and France to gain support as well as much needed funds. The pieces touched people the same way that holy relics of the past did, but these were relics of the future. The torch went to the Centennial Exposition in Philadelphia. Strategically, visitors were charged fifty cents to climb it, and the money went towards funding the pedestal. Philadelphia had played an instrumental role as a meeting place for the founding fathers of the United States. Their energy and their spirit still reside there.

The head with a crown, whose seven rays represent the seven continents, the seven seas, and, esoterically, the seven chakras leading to enlightenment, were displayed in a Parisian park. Then came a major test. A well-known laxative company offered to donate enough money to complete everything, if they could advertise on Liberty's head. Though the money was desperately needed, the offer was refused. It would have corrupted the very essence of what she stood for. Freeing the people from tyranny, which included the tyranny of advertising. After the offer was turned down, money started to roll in, in bits and pieces, up to the final hour.

In 1877, President Grant signed the bill designating Bedloe Island for the monument, agreeing that it would become a lighthouse. Celebrations ensued. It was all in order, as ordained from on high. A physical and symbolic lighthouse was born, but there was a growing dissidence in government, and they didn't want to contribute any more money. Joseph Pulitzer began a personal campaign in his paper New York World in an effort to raise more funds. It raised over one-hundred thousand dollars in six months:

"We must raise the money! The World is the people's paper, and now it appeals to the people to come forward and raise the money. The $250,000 that the making of the Statue cost was paid in by the masses of the French people – by the working men, the tradesmen, the shop girls, the artisans – by all, irrespective of class or condition. Let us respond in like manner. Let us not wait for the millionaires to give us this money. It is not a gift from the millionaires of France to the millionaires of America, but a gift of the whole people of France to the whole people of America."

In the end, the ordinary people of America financed the

foundation. Money came from penny donations from school children, and households giving under a dollar. Liberty was funded by the ordinary people, alchemically, exactly as it was meant to be. She was a statue for the people, and in the future, she would help to liberate them from another type of tyranny.

*

Richard Duchene's white cotton shirt stuck to his back from perspiration as he heated copper sheets in a scorching fire. A drop of sweat dripped from his brow, falling onto the metal, as he hammered and shaped the final sheet for the statue. On the final blow of a series of eight, he lifted his arm to strike. *The last strike of the last sheet, and it's finished*, he thought, before reciting the ancient Aramaic version of the Lord's Prayer, as was instructed. Someone shouted his name, and he missed his mark and struck his thumb. Cursing, he lifted the mallet, and to his horror, his thumbnail came off with it, blood dripping onto the copper from the oozing nail bed. The pain was excruciating. *I've now officially put my blood, sweat and tears into this project.* Holding his shirt between his teeth, he ripped a piece of cloth with his good hand, and wrapped it around his throbbing thumb. He fell to his knees, fearing he'd pass out from the pain. He cried out to the heavens. "Make it stop, Lord!" Then the pain was gone. He unwrapped his thumb, and the thumbnail was perfect again. Can this be so? Was it real, or was he hallucinating from the heat?

The droplets of blood on the copper shook as if the molecular structure was being charged, as if the blood was alive. Then it re-formed itself into the shape of Liberty's crown. Rubbing his eyes, Richard looked again. "Yes, it is the crown," he said out loud, before looking back at his thumb. "And yes. It is healed. Mon Dieux. C'est un miracle."

Any doubts about the project evaporated. It was heavenly

blessed. The gift to America, as Bartholdi had envisioned, would benefit mankind forever. He prostrated over the sheet, arms stretched to the sides like a crucifixion. He wanted to get as close to it, to her, as he could. Resting his cheek on the warm, dimpled surface, inhaling the ore, he could hardly keep awake, and drifted off into a vision. He was transported back to the ancient Sinai dessert. Hovering over a fire, a drop of sweat dripped from his brow onto the sand below. There was a growing queue of people handing him their precious gold items, earrings, bracelets, amulets, which he melted, and poured into moulds while repeating ancient Aramaic prayers. *Could it be true?* His heart cried as he realized it was he and another man who were constructing the Ark of the Covenant, the gold covered wooden chest to house the two stone tablets of the Ten Commandments. He watched as they dug up a mould and cracked it, gently revealing two golden cherubim facing each other with their arms held together in the shape of a vesica piscis.

"Aholiab!" a voice shouted. "Moses says we must continue on soon."

The shout woke him out of his dreamlike vision. He heated the sheet again, and curled a raw and blistered palm around the hammer. One final time, he raised his arm to the heavens, and struck the final blow. His task was complete. A task, he acknowledged, that was as significant as the Ark itself.

"Lady Liberty, what have I done to deserve two such honours in the reincarnation of my soul?" Richard asked the heavens. "Merci. Merci," he cried, over and over, placing the sheet on a barrow, and wheeling it over to the rest of the copper sheets.

"Richard!" the voice called again. "Monsieur Labouley est mort."

"Quoi?" he asked in disbelief.

A voice came over a megaphone. "Tout le monde. Aujourd'hui, c'est un triste jour. Nous avons perdu notre cher frère et le père de la Statue de la Liberté, Monsieur Labouley. Ayons le silence un moment."

The warehouse came to a standstill. There was a full minute of silence. Richard was in shock, despite hearing of Èdouard's stroke the night before. He was sure his comrade would recover. This was the final blow.

Later that evening, the lodge gathered in a ceremony, ensuring that Laboulaye's transition to the next world went gently and sweetly. They felt certain he was in the hands of the Goddess Liberty, and that his cycles of rebirth and karma were complete.

CHAPTER 16

ROSE COHEN & RICHARD DUNNE
The Avebury Complex
Present Day

"We're getting close," Paul, their tour guide, said as they passed through Devizes. Richard and Rose had heard word from some tourists at the hotel that a crop circle had appeared near Avebury the night before. The stone circle was already in their itinerary, so the crop circle was an added bonus. It was going to be their first stop after a full English breakfast at Polly's tearooms in Marlborough.

"Many crop circles appear on the plains and hills around this area and Wiltshire," Paul said. "Who, or what, makes them is unknown, but one thing's for sure, they have a funny energy. I've known watches and cameras to stop working inside them. Some people's photographs completely disappear!"

"What do you think about them?" Richard asked, slightly bemused by the whole thing.

"I've been doing these tours for over fifteen years. I've seen many things that are unexplainable. I think some of them are real, some aren't. If they're genuine, there's no damage to the crop. The wheat stalks simply bend over into a pattern, almost like they're bowing. The precision and intricacy of the patterns are incredible, impossible to make so quickly. They're known as temporary temples because they're formed with the principles of sacred geometry, like the great cathedrals and churches. You definitely feel different when you come out of one. I'm going to share a little secret. This is going to sound crazy, but I swear it's true. I was on a hill, not far from here. It was the end of a long day. The sun was going down. I'd been sitting looking over the fields to the horizon, peacefully contemplating life, when I looked down for a second. When I looked up again, there was a flash of light, and then, a crop circle appeared."

Rose gasped. "What did you do?"

"I've never moved so quickly! I grabbed my things and got the heck out of there! It was around sundown, and I was alone. They weren't gonna get me, the buggers."

Richard laughed. "I don't blame you!"

"I can't wait!" "We must get into the circle. Do you think we'll find it?"

"We'll find it. Whether you can get in is another story. The farmers can get a bit funny about people traipsing all over their crops, but we'll give it a good go," Paul said.

Shortly after, they pulled off the main road into a small lane in the village of Alton Barnes.

"Here we are. It should be about a fifteen-minute walk from that bridge going east. Follow the grass path. You can't miss it. It's near a small group of trees, the only ones around. I'll be back in a couple of hours. I'm going to grab a drink. Meet me back here at one."

After ten minutes of walking down a narrow grass path along a hedgerow, keeping to the side of a large field so they didn't damage any crops, a vast expanse of golden wheat and a clump of trees came into view, letting them know they were in the right place. Following along the horizon from the trees, led their eyes to the circle. It was huge. And humbling.

"I feel really small," Rose's voice cracked.

"I know what you mean."

They arrived at a sign at the edge of the field: Please keep to the tracks. The Farmer.

"We must be heading in the right direction," laughed Rose.

"It's interesting that they form so close to these ancient sites," Richard said, keeping the conversation light.

"Yeah. It's like past and future meet," Rose agreed following behind him along the path.

They were alone on the field. It was slightly eerie. Standing at the circle's outer edge, they already sensed something powerful. Rose was having heart palpitations, not the familiar anxiety ones, more like a stirring.

"Ready?" Richard asked.

"Ready."

They took a photograph, then they made their way to centre, laid out a blanket, and sat. "Do you feel like someone, or something knows we're here?"

"What, like we aren't alone?" Rose asked.

"Yeah. Something like that."

"I do feel like we are in the presence of the miraculous. Like it's working on us in a profound way."

They sat, faces towards the sun, absorbing the morning light. "This journey is just so different from anything I've ever experienced. I don't think I will ever be the same again. Thank you, Richard."

"For what?"

"For escorting me, or whatever you're doing here."

"Look at me, Rose. There is nothing to thank me for. We have been sent here together by my teacher.

'Rose was startled by a rustling sound in the wheat. A bird flew out of the stalks not far from them. Richard took Rose's hand in his, protectively, and lovingly. Then he ran his hand up the side of her arm, squeezing and caressing her elbow, her shoulder, and the back of her neck. Rose's heart beat quickly. Then holding her head in both of his hands, he pulled her into him, and kissed her.

Hesitant at first, she yielded to him slowly. She lay back on the ground, pulling him on top of her, enjoying the weight of his body. Both were eager to unite, as their passion for each other heightened. They held each other closer and closer, as if trying to merge their physical beings into one. It was as if their hearts were reaching out to seize the other's, striving to become one heart. Richard pulled back for a moment, and looked into Rose's eyes. She felt taken into another time and place. She felt it when their lips first met. This was not new love. In the distance, a bell tolled.

Richard pulled a twig out of Rose's hair, and drew her to him for one last kiss. "Come on. We'd better pull ourselves together."

Richard enlarged the picture of the crop circle on his phone. "Look at this, Rose," he said, tracing his finger along a pattern. "There's a star of David. And here, look, don't those spikes look like the crown of the Statue of Liberty?"

"Yes. It does. My God, Richard, you're right. It really does."

Richard grasped Rose's hand, and he led her around the circle. They traced each point as if they were connecting with a lost fragment of themselves.

"I feel reborn," Rose said.

"Me too," Richard agreed, holding her close, kissing her forehead, her nose, and finally her mouth, tenderly, as if she were a delicate flower.

Paul was there waiting when they returned. "What happened to you two? You're glowing!"

"On to Avebury!" Richard said, ignoring his question. "But first, can we visit that tomb you told us about on the way up? Feels right to go there first."

*

They pulled over onto the soft shoulder alongside a busy road. "I'll walk up with you, but I won't go in. I'm a bit claustrophobic."

"Really? I hate tight spaces too," Richard said.

"You'll be fine," Rose said. The sun was getting stronger so they took off their top layers, as they followed the path up to West Kennet Longbarrow.

"West Kennet is over five thousand years old. It was a very important burial chamber, not for the lay people, but for the high-ranking leaders of the clans. There are five rooms where noble families were buried. The highest ranking was buried at the very end. It's dark inside. There's a shaft of light that comes in through the top at the end chamber. People came to the tomb to communicate with their ancestors, sometimes thousands of years later. Maybe yours are there!" Paul laughed, after giving a bit of the site's history.

Rose met Richard's eye.

The entrance was like an opening into a birth canal of a great earthen womb. A candle flickered in the darkness, from the back chamber, and the smell of nag champa incense beckoned. Ethereal voices of women chanting permeated the space. It was especially powerful with the acoustics in the chamber.

"The river is flowing, flowing and growing, growing and flowing, back to the sea. Mother Earth carry me, your child I will always be..."

Walking towards the chanting, and the light at the end of the chamber, they came upon four women, hand in hand, singing, as they circled around a candle.

"Mother Earth carry me, your child I will always be, Mother Earth carry me back to the sea..."

Richard and Rose watched until one of ladies broke the chain and made a space for them to join. After a few rounds, they let go, and still singing, each lady greeted the two with warm smiles, and deep seeing eyes, as they exited.

Rose and Richard felt as if the 'Mother' had blessed them through these wise women.

Making their way back towards the car, Rose spotted a huge pyramid-like earthen mound in the distance. She felt drawn to its energy. "What's that?"

"That's Silbury Hill," Paul explained. "A manmade monument from Neolithic times. It's thought to be a fertility symbol to the Goddess. Experts think it may have been an ancient lighthouse. A fire would've been built on its top to guide visitors navigating the waterways. Others think it was like a giant battery with a metal monument on top, to attract lightning."

"This is just unbelievable," Richard said.

'Yes, it is,' Rose said. "And I must climb it."

The divine feminine felt closer to her each day. She was becoming a real entity, and Rose felt guided by Her presence, subtly operating in the background of her life. Rose felt Her illuminating the course she should take, just as She helped the ships navigate their course. This feminine energy wasn't a concept, but a reality, a consciousness.

"I hope you both don't mind, but I really feel a calling to climb Silbury Hill on my own. I promise I'll be quick."

"Well, I don't mind if you don't," Paul said to Richard.

"Of course not. Are you sure you don't want me to come with you?"

"I'll be fine, thank you," Rose said.

As she got closer to the monument, there was a 'No Entry' sign instructing not to proceed further, in order to prevent more damage to the delicate balance of fauna, and the structure of the hill. A wire fence surrounded it, but there was a hole where people had climbed through anyway. Rose walked up to the hole, and started to climb through, but stopped in her tracks. She was confused. On one hand, she felt the mother mound calling her, but she also felt the need to respect the sign. She sat down nearby to contemplate the course of action, and spoke to Her, as if She were a person.

"I'm confused," Rose said aloud. "I feel called to climb you. I long to know you." She stroked the grass between her fingers. "You are becoming real to me."

Suddenly the grass felt alive. Alive as if it were a sentient being. Rose felt as if she were in a symbiotic relationship with it.

"You are as close to me as possible, my dear daughter. The earth is my body. You needn't go anywhere. With the ground under your feet you are with me. You will find me in the rivers, the lakes, the oceans, the grass, the trees, and rocks. I feel when you care. I feel it when you stroke your fingers through me, and connect with me. Love me by developing your relationship with nature. Respect me, honour me, for I am what sustains your life. Spread this word, my lovely daughter. You are mine, always."

Rose realised that the world, which she'd previously inhabited, no longer existed. She had evolved to a whole new level of awareness, and she knew that with it came responsibility. In the shadow of an ancient hill, in the Wiltshire countryside, a city girl, born and bred, leant down and kissed the ground, and made a promise. As her lips touched the grass, she saw a flash of a giant radiant crystal inside the bottom of the hill, directly underneath an obelisk that stood on top.

She ran up to Richard by the car and threw her arms around him. "Thank you. Thank you. I have been blessed."

*

Paul dropped Rose and Richard at the processional avenue, which led into Avebury, the largest stone circle in Europe. "I'll meet you just where the avenue enters the main circle," he said, walking ahead and leaving them to enter by themselves.

Walking the avenue hand in hand, it felt as if they were walking down a church aisle, and the wedding party surrounding them were the stones, which also had a sentient quality. Some were distinctly male, and others female. Paul waited at the end like a reverend, arms outstretched, beckoning them to enter, guarded by two of the largest stones.

"This is a gateway. Before entering, acknowledge your past, acknowledge your stories, and everything and everybody that brought you here, the good and the difficult. Thank them, and then release. Make way for the new," Paul advised.

Without hesitation, Richard picked up Rose, spun her around, and shouted "Thank you!" at the top of his lungs, carrying her over a threshold.

"I now pronounce you man and wife!" Paul said, jokingly.

For the next three hours, they wandered, weaving in and out amongst the stones, touching, hugging, and listening to them, with a childlike innocence. They visited the points where the seasonal ceremonies took place, and performed a few of their own.

It was truly an internal banquet. At the end, they were full, whole and exhausted. Richard and Rose fell into the car and closed their eyes. When they opened them, they were five minutes from Glastonbury.

CHAPTER 17

ROSE COHEN & RICHARD DUNNE
The Abbey and the Chalice Well
Present Day

They woke several times throughout the night to make love. They got to know each other's secrets, heal past wounds, and patch up old hurts with each kiss. They completed, renewed, surrendered, let go, and united in the joy of union of man and woman. All of their fear evaporated.

In the morning, Rose woke first, with Richard's arm draped over her shoulder. She'd forgotten how nice it was to feel someone's body next to hers, and to wake up happy. And it wasn't just someone: it was her twin flame. She was a queen that had found her king. All the tormenting thoughts that usually occupied space in her mind simply weren't able to survive in the presence of love.

Richard mumbled a moment later, "Breakfast. Coffee. C'mon, up!" he jumped out of bed. "It's our last day. We have a lot to do!"

*

St. Margaret's Chapel, known by locals as the Magdalene Chapel, a tiny sanctuary dating from the mid-1400s, was empty of people, but full of peace when they entered. A well-worn red and gold Middle Eastern rug covered the floor.

Previous pilgrims had left offerings of dried flowers and lit tea light candles at one end. Rose placed some coins in the collection box and took another candle in her hand to offer her prayers to Mary Magdalene. Richard wrapped his hands around hers. They lit the candle, and left feeling calm, held, and blessed.

*

Acres of green manicured lawns carpeted the grounds of the remaining ruins of Glastonbury Abbey, once the richest monastery in England, according to the Domesday Book of 1086. Remnants of majestic buildings stood broken, but still proud, among ancient oaks, pines, yew, and maple trees.

Immediately sensing they were on holy ground, they prayerfully walked up the path, respecting the awesome presence they felt. Their awareness was acute, and they were receptive to the subtler realms. They were starting to recognise the energy permeating the entire mystical Isle of Avalon, which was especially noticeable there. It was almost physically tangible. Hand in hand they strolled, in silence, united in their reverence of whatever it was they perceived.

A dove flew into a crevice in the stones of the main building that housed the High Alter. Richard turned in its direction, and saw the subtle body of Ananda leaning against a yew tree, with his white robe and flowing hair, and a warm, glowing aura. The vision was gone in seconds. *He is always with me. Of course.*

Similar to many other churches and cathedrals all over Europe, the Abbey was built on an old pagan site, and was once an important Druid place of worship and initiation. The ancients knew to build where there were ley lines and vortexes. In those places, the veils between the worlds were thinnest, and the energy needed to transform was at its most potent.

Rose and Richard were particularly interested in the

legend that Jesus had come here with his great Uncle Joseph of Arimathea. They understood that he went through an initiation, and then built their first place of worship in the west – the Wattle Church – near the site of the current Mary Chapel. After the crucifixion of Jesus, Joseph was reputed to have brought relics, most notably the grail, back to Glastonbury to be hidden.

"Such a shame. Imagine what it was like before it was destroyed. Henry the Eighth has a lot to answer for," Rose said, breaking the silence.

"He must have been in a pretty unhappy marriage!" Richard replied. They both giggled, and then giggled at their giggling, which resulted in fits of laughter.

They walked around the duck pond, and stood on the wooden bridge that crossed it. They strolled through the apple orchard, and meandered through the herb garden learning about the plants used by the monks at the time for hygiene, medicine, and cooking. Rose picked a mint leaf and popped it in her mouth.

They went into the Abbot's Kitchen, the best preserved part of the Abbey. It was set out just like it was during the Abbey's heyday, with a wooden banquet table laid out with food that would have been served at a feast for the rich and wealthy pilgrims. A hefty man dressed as a monk, who looked like Friar Tuck, was giving a talk about life in the Abbey at the time.

Richard felt confused about his own journey and his future. He contemplated his life as a monk, the life he had chosen before meeting Rose. A simple existence consisting of eating, praying, worshipping with the other monks, as well as sharing the daily tasks of growing food, writing, and studying. He wondered where his life would lead after this journey. He wondered whether his future was with Ananda in India, or with Rose in New York. He dreaded having to make a choice, as both souls had so profoundly healed and fundamentally changed him. He certainly didn't want to hurt

Rose. She was a part of him now, and he a part of her, but Ananda had been his life, his reason to live for the past four years. His heart felt like it was breaking in two, and he understood the pain of separation.

"You don't have to choose, you know," Rose came up behind him and put her arms around his waist.

"What do you mean?"

"I mean, this experience has been the greatest blessing. I feel love, and am loved completely. I'm happy for the first time, and I understand what true unconditional love is. I want for you what is right for you. You are a monk, Richard. If you need to go back to India, of course I'll miss you, but I'll be ok. Knowing that you're happy, and that what we have is true and real and can never be broken is what's important to me."

Richard hung his head low.

"How did you know? It's as if you read my exact thoughts. We have a destiny together, Rose. I know it. We are being guided. We have been guided."

"I felt it since the moment I met you," Rose added, looking relieved that he felt the same.

"I've just remembered something. I had the most incredible dream last night. Ananda took both our hands, and was leading us around somewhere – here I think! It was a tremendous blessing. He said that Glastonbury is the heart chakra of the planet, and then he embraced us both. He told us that in this life our work was in the world, but that I would come back to India. It was a fatherly love. We are being guided, Rose, to do something together in this world, complete an agreement we made. A door has opened in my heart."

"That's a wonderful dream, Richard."

Richard could sense Rose had tried in earnest to show her joy, but he could also detect sadness when he said he would return to India.

The Friar Tuck monk turned towards them, swinging his

metal goblet around.

"Alfred Grimsby?" Rose said above the crowd. His one eye turned towards them.

"Well, hello. If it ain't my drinking buddies from the pub!" he said, putting down the goblet. "I volunteer here a few days a week. Don't go telling anyone now. It'd ruin my reputation. How are you enjoying yerselves?"

"We're great," Richard answered.

Alfred noticed something had changed between them. "Ah, I think Merlin's magic is working its wonders on ye. Come. I want to show you something you won't find in the guidebook." He led them out the door.

"See that there stone? It's called the egg-stone. An archaeologist, Frederick Blighe Bond was his name, communicated with dead monks. They still walk around the Abbey, by the way, and drink in the pub like I told you already. Anyway, he discovered it through automatic writing in the early 1900s. He was told to excavate behind the high altar. And lo and behold there was this ancient stone! Just look at it."

"Must weigh over two hundred pounds," Richard said, staring at it.

"Must be over two hundred pounds?" Alfred muttered. "Is that all you have to say? This here's a druid's stone, used for ritual and ceremony by the ancient wise people. My people," he winked with his good eye. "But don't tell 'em here in the abbey that I told you. They'll have me hung, drawn and quartered on the Tor, just like that unfortunate Abbot Whiting, last Abbot of Glastonbury. See that indentation?"

"Yes. Why is it shaped like that?" Rose asked.

"That's the chalice. That there is the most important relic in this Abbey, and no one knows. It's hidden right here, in plain sight. See how it's red in the bowl? That's from blood."

"Why is it so important? Was it for sacrifices?"

"That, my dear, is a good question. In the days of olde,

before organised religion, the feminine was honoured through the power of the healing flow. At certain times of the year, be it yer solstices or yer equinoxes, the maiden offered the blood of her womb. She put it in the cup of the stone or chalice. Now don't ask me any details, mind. That's women's business. Anyway, shaped like an egg of fertility, people would form a procession like to receive a blessing. This here stone and the flow of blood was the connection between the worlds. Here and the hereafter. These traditions were kept alive in the early Celtic Church. But when them Romans took over, well they nearly drove everything underground. Literally! Suppressed it all. The symbols were buried or destroyed with them, or adapted for their own purposes, so they could get control of the people and the sites. Where do you think the chalice that held the blood of Christ came from? The olde ways are coming back."

"You're a strange man, Arthur Grimsby," Richard said.

"Me? Never met anything stranger than a man, or a monk that didn't partake in ablutions! The monks here got a pitcher of ale a day. Kept 'em going. Put hair on their chests," he said, winking at Rose.

Alfred suddenly took on a very serious demeanour, and his voice dropped to a whisper. "We are entering an age when the sacred feminine is being restored." He took out a small bottle and he turned to Richard. "Don't worry. It's only water. Blessed water." He poured it into the bowl of the stone, and told them both to put two fingers into the water and then sprinkle it over the other. They did as they were told, and Alfred roared with laughter. "That there's a fertility rite you've just done! Now go on you two. The high altar is over there. Go stand on it. Never mind about them chains. It's a gateway, where the Mary and Michael lines cross. See what happens. And make your last stop the healing waters of Chalice Well, where the two ley lines cross again, the perfect balance of male and female."

Without another word, Arthur bowed, and walked away.

As they walked towards the high altar, it was as if a current of energy, a magnetic force, carried them. It stopped just between the high altar and the resting places of Arthur and Guinevere, so they stayed there.

Richard saw the ley lines illuminate in front of them and around them one by one, as if they were standing in the centre of the sun with rays beaming outward. They both heard Ananda's voice.

"You've made it. You are standing on the holiest of holy spots, the epicentre of the heart chakra. My children, the heart is the grail and the gateway between heaven and earth. You've healed your hearts. Now the perfect balance of male and female, together and separate, your work is to help re-establish this balance on earth," Ananda's voice faded. "Blessings upon you."

Richard grabbed Rose enthusiastically.

"Rose, I've got it! Remember, the first person to see Jesus after the crucifixion was Mary Magdalene, proving that she was the closest to him spiritually, and the link between heaven and earth. She was the one that led him to the room where the disciples were, and proved there is no death. Then the Roman Church concealed all of the references to the Magdalene healing power in order to suppress the feminine. We are part of the reawakening of the divine feminine! I'm not sure how or why, but I know it!"

He pulled her to the High Altar. "Come on, Rose," he said, dragging her over the chained off area with such enthusiasm that she nearly fell.

"This is a vortex," Rose said, as she stepped over the chain and stood at the altar.

"Rose, wait." A series of pictures appeared in Richard's mind, and he described what he saw.

"I'm in the desert. I've got dark skin and a beard. I am with another man and we are wearing cloth robes, almost like sacks. We have long metal clamps in our hands. We are working over a kiln built in the ground. There's a line of people giving us their gold, the rings off of their fingers even, their most precious wedding bands. We are melting them for something very important, reciting prayers as we do it. What? I'm being shown the Ark of the Covenant! I'm making the Ark of the Covenant? I'm being taken somewhere else now, to a later time. I'm in a huge building, like an aircraft hangar. There are lots of people dressed in old fashioned clothing, but I'm seeing it in black and white. We are speaking French. Wait, I'm seeing the same scene I saw in the Statue of Liberty when I was chiselling the date 1776 on her tablet. I know we are working on something very important, not everyone knows how important it is, but I do. Hang on. I'm talking to someone. I'm very serious. I have tools in my hand. Now I'm making the sheets of copper that will form Liberty's body." Richard heard the word 'alchemist' in his inner ear. "I'm an alchemist, Rose." He took her hand. "I'm hammering the metal, and I'm saying a prayer, the same prayer I said when I built the Ark, and I'm concentrating on the number of times I am pounding into this copper. It seems very important to me. I have been given a very important task, one given from above. Yes, I have to hammer in sets of eight blows, no more, no less. We are using copper because its alchemical symbol is the same as that of Venus, the divine feminine," Richard tilted his head with his left ear up towards the sky. "I'm saying the Lord's prayer in Aramaic. A man is coming in. I greet him with a secret handshake. Bartholdi? He shows me a plan and takes me, and my piece of metal, into another part of the hall. Oh my God, Rose! It's amazing. It's the head of the Statue of Liberty! We're working on building the crown of the Statue of Liberty!"

Richard took in a deep breath. Rose held the space for his process, anchoring his experience.

"I'm in a secret meeting room. It's the same era. I've just fainted. I'm lying on the floor, with a white and purple beaded belt in my hand. There is an incredible presence of love in the room. I'm surrounded by a group of men, and a flood of angelic light is filling the room. A presence is talking through me! I couldn't hear then, but I can hear now." Richard repeated the words aloud. "This vehicle which I now inhabit has been given a mission from on high as we are about to enter the final phase of the earth's evolution. He has the alchemical knowledge, experience, and purity of heart, and devotion to carry out this most important task. Richard Duchene will esoterically encode the gift that Bartholdi will design for the United States. This gift is much more than meets the eye, much more than a symbol. It will help awaken humanity. When the time is right, Richard will reincarnate in the United States, and will, with his female counterpart, fully activate the codes."

As he came back into the now, their journey together became clear, as well as the roles of all the people that had crossed their path, guiding them, and all the events which led them to where they currently stood.

"Rose, from the moment I met you there was a spark of recognition. What scared me was what the spark would ignite. I'm so glad I've overcome that fear. When I was in India, I had many doubts. I knew I was changing, but honestly, I was apprehensive about the life of a renunciate. Ananda was right to push me out. I know why he did now, and how right it is. In finding you, I have found myself. In walking through the gates of the heart to allow myself to love you, I have opened the door to know myself." Running his fingers through her hair, clutching the back of her head, he looked into her being, and then lifted her off the ground.

With a smile on her face and a hand on her heart, she launched into an emotional rendition of 'My Country 'Tis of Thee'. It was a song that Rose sang first thing every morning in grade school, following the Pledge of Allegiance:

"My country, 'tis of thee, Sweet land of liberty, Of thee I sing; Land where my fathers died, Land of the pilgrims' pride, From ev'ry mountainside Let freedom ring!"

She shook her head. "I don't know why that hymn just popped into my head. I've always loved it, even more than the pledge. I never really understood the real meaning of that song until now. I'm ready to go home, Richard."

*

The entrance to the Chalice Well Healing and Meditation Garden was through a pergola covered in climbing roses and honeysuckle, lined with hanging baskets of fuchsias, begonias, pansies and geraniums. It was like entering the Garden of Eden, or a romantic era painting by J. W. Waterhouse. It was as if Summer herself were blessing them, and secretly, inside her being, Rose knew Mother Nature's blessings to be true. Hand in hand, they stopped to admire a mosaic artwork of two interlocking circles, near the entrance.

"That's familiar," Rose commented.

A silver-haired woman with dazzling blue eyes and a bright smile stood at the gatehouse entrance.

"Are you two companions?" she asked.

"Yes, we are travelling together," Richard replied.

"No, I mean are you members of the Well already?" She laughed. "I presume not," she said handing him a leaflet. "Would you like to buy a bottle to fill with the waters?"

"Okay sure, we'll take a small one," Rose said.

The gentle, soothing, and relaxing sounds of flowing water and birdsong accompanied them, as they explored the multi-levelled gardens. They began at the lowest lawn, where once again the two interlocking circles pattern formed a shallow pool, which caught a heavy stream of running water before it flowed across the lawn, then disappeared underground through a pipe at the end of the garden.

"Richard, the two interlocking circles *again*."

"It's obviously the symbol for the Chalice Well, Rose. It's everywhere."

"I know, but what does it mean?"

Richard shrugged his shoulders. A small crowd of women and a male tour guide assembled nearby.

"This is a sacred spring. Has been for thousands of years. An average of twenty-five thousand gallons of water flows daily, at a consistent temperature and velocity throughout. Its source is unknown, but most likely comes from underneath the range of hills you see in the background, the Mendips. There's been reputed healings from this water, going back hundreds of years, perhaps thousands, probably due to its iron rich waters. See the stains it has left? You can also taste it when we fill our bottles on the third level up."

The ladies hung on to his every word.

"Although the Well has been here for thousands of years, it was only through the efforts of the mystic visionary, Wellesley Tudor Pole, that a trust was formed to safeguard the Well's future, enabling it to serve as a place of pilgrimage once again. That house behind you there is a retreat house. I highly recommend a few days there. But you can only stay if you become a companion."

"*That's* what the lady at the gatehouse meant when she asked if we were companions. Of the Well. We're coming back," Rose said, nudging Richard.

The guide continued. "On the top floor of the house, the Upper Room is laid out as a replica of the last supper. It used to house the Blue Bowl, an ancient bowl that Mr Pole received in a vision. It was found buried at St. Brides Well here in Glastonbury. He was guided to send the bowl to sacred sites around the world, forming an energy connection between them. Many people receive inspiration from the gardens, but also in that Upper Room. There are certain times when visitors and companions can go up to meditate. The spirit guardians of Glastonbury work profoundly in it. The idea for Scotland's Findhorn came as guidance while Peter and Eileen Caddy meditated in that room. I've been coming here for thirty years. I've seen custodians come and go, but I feel one couple deserves to be mentioned."

"Wow. He sure can talk! Hasn't even taken a breath!" Richard said.

"Shhh, Richard. I'm trying to listen."

"While living at Findhorn, Willa and Leonard Sleath got an invitation to come here and run the Well. They didn't want to return, but Willa had a reading which confirmed the rightness. Willa felt instinctively that something wasn't right about this section at the bottom. She's responsible for opening it up creating this free flow water sculpture that leads into the pool. It used to just go underground. The sculpture mimics the natural flow of water, charges it as it streams from chamber to chamber within the structure. As the momentum builds, it flows over the edge. It's almost like the birth canal."

The ladies all agreed, and supported his theory.

"Now, the vesica piscis shape. This pool the water pours into is one of the most sacred symbols in the world."

Rose elbowed Richard to make sure he was paying attention.

"It's found all across the world. There's even a theory that the two cherubim on the lid of the Ark of the Covenant held a vesica piscis between them."

Richard and Rose were transfixed. The hand of destiny was surely weaving synchronicity into the fabric of their lives.

"What does the vesica piscis mean?" a lady with a strong southern drawl asked.

"There are many theories. Many say the space in the middle of the two interlocking circles became the fish symbol for Christ, and others say it's the inspiration for the arches in Chartres Cathedral. Actually, that space in the middle is a representation of balance, of male and female, of the yin and yang, heaven and earth meeting, the flower of life and creation."

The hairs on Rose's arm stood on end, and she showed Richard, who was experiencing the same thing.

"The ancient people worshiped around holy wells. This place has been used by the ancient Celts for thousands of years, and still today, their presence remains. Modern day pilgrims come on the old pagan festivals, equinoxes and solstices, and full moons. It's still a living space, even more so now, as more and more people turn back to the old ways and seek connection with Mother Earth to find an understanding of the complexities in modern life. To find simplicity. Now let's continue. Follow me."

"This whole place feels like a perfect ending to our journey. I wonder if there's a possibility of getting into the Upper Room before we go," said Rose.

"We'll ask on the way out. Let's go fill our bottles."

The garden felt multi-dimensional and very protected. Everything was perfect, growing as Mother Nature herself would have them, unlike the manicured lawns of a country estate. One could almost see the fairies dancing and skipping lightly over the waters, or hiding shyly behind fern leaves.

In Arthur's Court, trees shaded a trickling waterfall, which streamed into a wading pool, a welcome relief on a hot day. A scent of lavender travelled on a gentle breeze between them. Rose took off her shoes and stepped into the water to cool off, nearly slipping on the iron-covered slick surface of the bath.

"It's cold!" she shouted, grabbing onto the edge for stability.

Afterward, they rested under an arbour, where they were offered a perfect view of the Lion's Head fount. Visitors of all ages and nationalities were lined up there to sample the waters. They supped the sacred spring, savouring its healing properties as the cool water trickled down their throat.

The whole experience was teaching Rose about the regenerative force of nature. It soothed and calmed and touched her at a deep level. In a very short week, in the Somerset countryside, she had learnt to appreciate its rhythm, and its calming influence. She didn't experience anxiety anymore, she felt in balance. "Respect me, honour me, for I am what sustains your life. Spread this word, my lovely daughter," the words repeated in her mind.

When there was a lull in the line, they approached the wellspring. Richard filled the bottle, gave it to Rose, and then filled his own. They looped their arms around the other, and drank. Everything seemed to flow effortlessly, like the spring itself.

They proceeded up the path, where flowers were planted like chakras, colours from red up to violet, culminating at the entrance to the wellhead. Rose pointed to a sign: *Please Observe Silence. People in Meditation and Prayer.*

Taking a seat around the holy well, they joined a barefoot elderly woman with dyed purple and red hair. She wore silver rings, and ribbons, and a necklace of crystals and feathers.

Must be one of the modern day pagans, Rose thought to herself.

"Leave something for the Goddess before you go. She will guide and protect you on your path. Something of you, a peace of hair, a bit of fingernail."

"I guess it can't hurt," Richard said. They both plucked a hair, and dropped it down the cavernous hole.

*

"I'm sorry, the Upper Room is only open to visitors on certain days of the week, and certain times," said the gatekeeper.

"Oh, that's disappointing. Not meant to be I guess," Rose replied. She and Richard started walking to the exit, but were stopped by a woman passing by.

"Excuse me, I couldn't help but overhear that you wanted to go into the Upper Room. I'm staying at the Little St. Michael retreat house. We have access all day. I can take you up as my guests, if you like," she said.

"That would be terrific! Thanks," Richard said.

Rose felt instantly at home in the cottage. It was everything she dreamed an English country cottage would be – cosy and quaint, with pained windows and little nooks full of books.

"That's Wellesley Tudor Pole," the woman said, pointing to a bronze bust on the bureau.

Rose stopped to admire it, and pay her respects.

On the second level with the bedrooms, the energy started to change, peace and deep silence were tangible, and only got stronger as they ascended a final staircase.

"Enjoy your time. It's a special place," the lady said, opening the door for them to enter.

It felt like they were entering a holy temple or church, as if many prayers had been offered there *and* many prayers had been heard. The air was charged with spiritual presence.

The room was divided into two parts. One side was an area for meditation and contemplation, and behind a partition was a recreation of the last supper. Richard put his arm around Rose's shoulder. There was an intense heat emanating from her backpack. "Rose, take off your backpack. It's like something's on fire in there!"

"It's the relic from Templecombe!" Rose said, scrambling through the pockets to retrieve it. It practically jumped out of the cotton handkerchief, and rolled onto the floor, stopping underneath a cabinet. "Grab it!"

"It's trying to tell us something," Richard said, climbing over the partition to recover the relic. As he got closer, he felt an undeniable impulse to open the cabinet. To his astonishment, inside was the Blue Bowl. He carefully lifted it out, and held it gently for a moment. He then placed it in the centre of the wooden table, directly in front of where Christ would have sat, and softly positioned the relic inside it. Immediately he felt the auras of both holy objects merge. After a few minutes, he returned the bowl to the cabinet and climbed back over to Rose.

"I don't know how long we'll have alone in here. Should we meditate?" Rose whispered.

"Rose, look at that," Richard said pointing to a plaque next to a candle left for visitors. 'Somewhere within the soul, there is silence. Attain unto it. It is a pearl of great price.'"

Sitting side by side, faces towards the warm sunshine beaming through the window panes, they shut their eyes to attain the silence, and the pearl.

Several minutes passed before Rose heard Ananda's voice. "I've always been here, but now that the doors of perception are opening within you, our contact will be much more powerful. I will be working with you for the remainder of your life on the inner plains."

Rose felt a tingling vibration in her heart centre. "The return of the feminine principle will start in America. The fullness of the feminine aspect was established there from the beginning. She is the essence of America, the Divine Feminine. She will usher in a new age of freedom. You are a key."

*

Richard also heard Ananda's voice.

"In the near future, after the crown chakra is fully activated, people will work with the energy that Liberty carries, at the highest level. You and Rose embody the keys and codes, carried through your lifetimes and genetics. You are now ready to fulfil your destiny in this final phase of earth's evolution towards higher consciousness."

In Richard's third eye, a queue of people formed from times past. Great thinkers, philosophers, artists, writers and politicians. They were souls who had received the inspiration to paint or draw, or start new businesses after ascending Liberty. He could feel them all giving him their blessing.

Ananda's voice continued, "In a very short time, a country that started with nothing became the most powerful country in the world. The energy of the crown chakra sped things up, but America has lost its way. It has become a nation of fear and control. But it is certain that She will soon take her rightful place once again as the most powerful nation on earth. Remember, it is not power that comes with position, but true power. The founding fathers established it in the Declaration of Independence:

"We hold these truths to be self-evident, that all men are created equal, that they are endowed by their Creator with certain unalienable Rights, that among these are Life, Liberty and the pursuit of Happiness."

"True freedom, true power, and true *liberty*, is knowing oneself beyond the mind and body. With it comes non-attachment, and a peace that no person, place or thing can give, or take away. In previous ages, most people who opened their crown chakra could not remain on earth. The frequency of the planet was too dense, and the only way they could survive was to go into the wilderness or away from society. Now, consciousness is being made ready, and spiritual principles are being integrated. The lower chakras of karma are being worked through quickly, and the higher chakras are being activated. Those that open their crown chakra now can and will remain here to fulfil their missions. As more and more people begin working with the higher chakras, especially as they activate their crown, the darkness that seeks to keep humanity from finding their spiritual destiny will surface. Institutions that keep us slaves to debt, or governments that seek control through manipulation, regardless of the cost to humanity, or the earth, will be exposed. In the presence of light, there is no darkness. Anything that appears as separation and division will come to light, anything hidden will be exposed. For a period of time it will feel as if the dark is overwhelming, and it will get worse for a time. But the crown chakra is divine light. It will prevail."

"Now open your eyes," Ananda said to them both at the same time. Standing before them, was Ananda's etheric body, his piercing eyes staring at them. He held his palms up towards them, as if giving a blessing. "Your journey is about finding freedom. Here in Glastonbury, the heart chakra, you have found your spiritual and human destinies, which are always intertwined in service. Go back to Liberty now, and complete the ascension to the crown together."

Ananda touched them both on the tops of their heads, and then his etheric body faded.

No words were necessary. Speaking felt like an intrusion, even their own thoughts felt like an intrusion. They knelt around the candle, bowing their heads, and then blew out the flame as if blowing the past away.

When they stepped out of the room, they were stepping into their destiny, as one.

CHAPTER 18

RICHARD DUCHENE
Liberty Island, New York
August 1884 – October 1886

The day had finally arrived. August 5th, 1884. Bartholdi and Richard Duchene, along with a hundred members of the grand lodge of New York, and municipal leaders from the across the nation, were ferried to Bedloe Island to lay the cornerstone in the foundation of Lady Liberty's pedestal. The cornerstone, the first stone set in the construction of a masonry foundation, was extremely important, physically and symbolically.

Nothing could dampen the spirit of the day, not even the torrential downpour. Bartholdi and Duchene watched proudly as an army band played the French National Anthem. A full Masonic ceremony ensued, including the handing over of tools to the Grand Master, who passed them on to other members of the lodge. The Grand Secretary then read a list of special items to be placed inside a copper box, inside the cornerstone, a sacred time capsule: a copy of the US Constitution, George Washington's farewell address, twenty bronze medals of former US Presidents, copies of New York City newspapers of the day, a poem on Liberty, a list of the Grand Lodge Officers, and, to Bartholdi's extreme delight, a portrait of himself, but perhaps the single most important item was Gela of the Lenape tribe's wampum belt, the very same belt left by George Washington in the ectoplasm on that fateful day. In that moment, by that act, the karmic debt of the original settlers of New York was made right. Gela, the spirit of Liberty, the matriarch of Manhattan, gave her blessing.

"Square, level and plumb!" the Grand Master declared, as he struck three blows with the gavel and confirmed the stone duly laid, before consecrating it with corn, wine, and oil: the fruit of the land, the brew of the grape and the essence of the olive – a homage to the Masons who built Solomon's temple, who were paid with those precious items of the day.

*

The Statue of Liberty was dismantled in Paris, packed into cases, and shipped to New York. It arrived in June, 1885. It then took more than a year to reassemble for her dedication on October 28th, 1886.

This was a national event of the greatest proportions, and was declared a public holiday in the city. People came to Manhattan in droves; every hotel was filled to capacity. The people of New York let loose. They were hanging out of office and apartment windows, throwing confetti that Wall Street workers had made from the paper of the updated brokerage results from the ticker tape machines. It was the birth of the ticker tape parade. Grand Marshal Charles P. Stone, led twenty thousand people in a parade. Many of them were members of Masonic Lodges. The procession started at 57th Street, passed President Cleveland's stand at Madison Square Park, and continued to the Battery, where groups were once again taken by ship to Bedloe's Island.

*

Bartholdi was given the fitting job of lifting the tri-coloured

French flag to reveal Liberty's face. Before beginning his climb up the statue, for the official unveiling, he took a moment to acknowledge everything that had led him to this day. He reviewed all the obstacles, and all the challenges they'd faced to bring Lady Liberty to physical reality: the financial, political, practical and logistical problems. His thoughts turned to Laboulaye, and that auspicious dinner gathering all those years ago. He was sorry that his friend was not with him, after all, the idea had been his inspiration. His absence wasn't entirely surprising, as Laboulaye had shared a premonition that he wouldn't see her birth, and even hinted that he would support Bartholdi from behind the veils.

As he climbed, Bartholdi reminisced about his vision of Liberty poised at the gateway of the harbour all those years ago. Now she was complete, a physical manifestation of an energy that had already existed there. It took so many years to come to fruition. Yet he knew the timing was right, and that the challenges were part of the process. The gestation period in the womb was now complete.

Step by step, he ascended Liberty, considering what she meant to France, to America, and to the world. He contemplated what she represented now, and what was to come in the future. Calm, centred, and complete, he made his way to his destination.

Once inside, he anticipated the moment when he would pull the rope that would remove the large French flag, unveiling Liberty's face. Looking down to her left hand holding the tablet with the date of the Declaration of Independence, he felt a surge of pride, and waited as Count Ferdinand de Lesseps gave his speech. There was a gun salute, music, and the statue was formally presented to the President of the United Sates, President Cleveland. Bartholdi gave his thanks to the Lord, and pulled the rope with all his might. A hush came over the crowd, followed by a huge round of applause.

The program was closed with a benediction pronounced

by Bishop Potter.

"The Statue of Liberty is not just a colossal two hundred and twenty-five ton pile of metal reaching some three hundred feet in the air at the entrance of New York Harbour, conspicuous by day and a guide to mariners by night. Magnificent in its conception, wonderful in design, and a masterpiece of engineering skill, this gigantic figure, holding aloft a torch of freedom in one hand and clasping a book of laws inscribed with the date 'July 4, 1776' in the other, casts its light far beyond the horizon. The light which illumines the Statue of Liberty is a guiding symbol to the path of freedom for men of all nations."

Bartholdi felt that if he died in that moment, he'd die a happy man. His life's purpose was complete. He was sure that he felt the presence of Laboulaye, like a midwife, pulling the rope with him, cutting the umbilical cord. Liberty was born.

Liberty's torch was lit for the first time that chilly autumnal evening. Bartholdi didn't feel the cold as he stood on the edge of the east side of New York City, viewing it in the distance. He thought about the day at the lodge, when the angel came, and said that his dear friend Richard Duchene would reincarnate in the future, and activate her to her full potential: "The people who pass through, will go through an alchemical process that will lead them towards enlightenment, and attain spiritual freedom. No longer will they be slaves, physically or spiritually. They will be free."

His heart was full as he contemplated the meaning of those words. The ascension process. Alchemy. Base chakra to the crown, like base metal into gold. Liberty is in situ, waiting for the right time, when people are ready for the final phase of the earth's evolution.

Liberty was a Trojan Horse hiding a most powerful secret – the end of the grail quest. She was hidden in plain sight.

CHAPTER 19

RICHARD, ROSE & SAMUEL
New York City
Present Day

"Damn!" Elizabeth yelled, jiggling the mouse on the pad in effort to wake it. "It's frozen again," she said sliding her office chair away from the desk. "I can't stand it anymore!"

Samuel knew the mouse was not the real issue. It was frustrating, yes, but she wasn't normally so bothered by things like that. "We don't have to do this, you know," Samuel said, taking his wife's arm to calm her down.

"Yes, we do," she answered, momentarily lowering her head into her hands. "Look at you. You're an old man, and I'm an old woman. We're tired. If only Rose..." she stopped her sentence halfway.

"Would, could, or *wanted* to take over?" Samuel finished for her. He switched off her computer, and sat by her side. "She doesn't want to, and she can't. And it's ok. We're gonna be great. We've earned our time to relax, and enjoy each other while we still have our health."

"Selling is so... final. We've put our lives into this business. Your parents put theirs. It's our family home. And I don't think *I'm* ready," she said emphatically.

"If we sell, we will have the money to live more than comfortably, *and* Rose will be secure for the rest of her life, so will generations to come. If there ever is another generation," he added without much hope.

The business and its assets had been appraised that morning. The real estate alone would put them well into the millionaire's club, many times over.

Some years back, they'd purchased a large lakefront property in Connecticut in need of renovation. It was a labour of love that they'd been refurbishing little by little. It was close to nature, and a peaceful place to retire. The house had a special feeling, and the location was simply magical, surrounded by mature trees, with a view across the lake. It also had five bedrooms, enough for any amount of family and friends. Of utmost importance was the fact it was close enough to the city, and Rose. When they'd bought it, they'd still had hope that Rose and Adam would take Maison over. Those plans quickly went awry.

They were apprehensive about telling Rose of their decision to sell. They had gone ahead with it without her input to relieve her of any sense of responsibility or guilt.

*

Rose nudged her backpack with her foot under the seat in front to make sure it was still there. After all, it contained the holiest of holy relics guarded by her ancestors for centuries. She held Richard's hand to calm his nerves for the imminent landing.

"It's amazing. I'm not afraid anymore. No claustrophobia, or anxiety," he said. "But I'll take that beautiful hand anyway," he said, lifting her hand in his after retrieving a box from the Chalice Well from his pocket. He looked into Rose's eyes.

"Our time in Glastonbury has been life-changing for both of us, I think," he said, searching her face for validation.

He removed a ring from the box. Rose's heart raced. *Is this a gift or a proposal?* She admired the delicate silver band with a vesica piscis design.

"Rose, our time together was more than I could ever have dreamed. I want you in my life, always. I want to wake up next to you, touch your hair, smell your perfume, and look into those gorgeous eyes."

Rose felt lifted out of the ordinary, as if his words were penetrating layers of her being that hadn't been touched in lifetimes.

"These have been the most joyous times of my life, on every level. My heart feels like it is being pulled out of me." Rose held his hand tighter. "Bottom line, I love you."

He slid the ring onto her wedding ring finger, and held her head close, as he nuzzled his face into her neck, kissing her all the way up to her ear.

"Marry me?"

"Yes! Yes!" Rose repeated with all of her being.

"Passengers on the left, look out of your window. There's a marvellous view of the Manhattan skyline. Keep your eye out for the Statue of Liberty," the captain announced.

*

Richard was on the phone to Edith the minute they got into the cab. Rose was on the phone to her family, bringing them up-to-date.

The plan was that they would both go back to Rose's apartment, and they'd meet everyone the day after next for a late breakfast at Maison at eleven. First, they had to complete something, as per Ananda's instructions at Edith's dinner party, which now seemed a lifetime ago.

Edith couldn't wait to see them. She'd already had an email saying much had happened, but was worried about Rose hearing the news of her parents selling Maison.

Richard ran from room to room with a youthful exuberance, and couldn't contain his excitement when he saw the views from Rose's apartment. "This one's mine!" he declared when he stepped into the master bedroom, "but if you're a good girl I'll share with you," he laughed, pouncing on her bed. Rose jumped on top of him, straddling his legs and holding his arms down.

"Stop. Get off. I can't stand being trapped," he shouted, squirming out from under her.

"What's the magic word?"

"Abracadabra?"

"Nope." She held on tighter.

"Pretty please, with sugar on top?"

"Um... Nah."

"Rose, I'm stronger than you," he said playfully, lifting her with his hips, throwing her over, and straddling her.

"Hey! That's not fair."

Richard leaned in closer, and looked into her eyes. "What's not fair?"

She leaned up to kiss him. He moved in closer, but instead of kissing him, she blew a raspberry on his neck, and wriggled out from under him. The two lay sideways on the bed, catching their breath.

"Remember at Edith's when Ananda told us that we were to fully open the 'doors' of the statue of Liberty?" Rose asked. "He said that we'd find our way. All I know is, I got clear guidance at Templecombe that I had to bring the piece of the relic of John the Baptist to the Statue of Liberty, and to leave it there."

Richard nodded in agreement. "Remember he also said we had to go through the ascension process together, which would culminate in the crown? Well, I think that was literal! We'll go through our own physical ascension process together while we make the climb up Liberty's chakras to her crown." All of the pieces were finally coming together. "Rose, remember Ananda saying that we both carry something in our DNA?"

"Yes."

"Think about it. What have we discovered? All our

previous lives are linked through incarnations and DNA. I am a descendant of the original stonemasons of the Ark of the Covenant, and carried that knowledge of encoding to the Statue of Liberty. You are a descendant of the original Knights Templar on your mother's lineage, as well as the first priests in the Temple of Jerusalem on your father's! When the time and age is right, opportunity is given to fulfil our destiny. The time is now."

"I'm not going to sleep tonight," Rose said, feigning exhaustion.

"No, you are not, and neither am I," Richard winked.

But they did sleep, body to body. All was perfect. Nothing to yearn for. Nothing to worry about. No angst or turmoil. Just a deep, life-affirming rest.

On the subway the next day, Richard recalled the incident with Miguel, wondering what had happened to him, and if his life had turned around. He'd seen Ananda turn around so many lives, including his own.

The journey to the statue was effortless, as if carried on a current of grace. Even the weather was gorgeous. The ferry ride was smooth, and the line to get in moved quickly, almost too quickly. Richard and Rose both had nervous anticipation. It was the unknown. What would happen? Why were they there? They only knew that it was the right time to be there. Something would be triggered in them, or by them, or both.

"It's changed so much since I was last here," Rose said. "You never used to have to leave your belongings before. Must be since 9/11," she added, shutting the locker. "Wait!" She fumbled through the inner pockets of her backpack, and found the antique handkerchief. "Phew! I almost forgot this!" she said, tucking it into her bra for safekeeping.

The place was jam-packed, but people didn't seem to know they were there, didn't acknowledge them, or even bump into them. It was as if they were on another frequency, or moving in another dimension.

In complete trust, like two innocent babes in the womb,

they began their ascent to be reborn.

As they climbed, Rose felt the holy relic at her chest vibrating, as if it were coming alive, being activated. "We must be close," Rose said, putting Richard's hand on her heart so he could feel energy coming from her.

Breathless, they finally reached the spiral staircase. Rose stepped onto the first step and held the metal rail. "Do you feel that?"

"Sure do," Richard replied, holding up a goose-pimpled arm while running his mala beads through his fingers.

"I feel lightheaded, as if my mind is shutting down, or turning off, or – I can't explain," Rose said.

"I know. I feel it too, like I'm about to jump out of an airplane, or something."

"Yes, exactly," she took a deep breath, "It's like we're jumping into another reality!"

"A double helix," a voice said to them both.

"Did you hear that?" Richard questioned.

"Yes."

"I'm Gela of the Lenape."

Rose repeated out loud to Richard, "Gela," and Richard interrupted – "of the Lenape." Confirming that they were both hearing the same voice.

"Remember this pattern from your human biology. The double helix stranded molecules of DNA contain all the information of the human body," the voice continued.

"Yes," they answered in unison. Rose looked back at Richard behind her.

"The dormant part of the genetic code is being activated. This staircase is Liberty's etheric pineal gland, the door to the multi-dimensionality in the human body, a link between the physical and spiritual worlds. From now on, when visitors walk this staircase, their own DNA will be activated, opening the doors of perception through their third eye. The pituitary gland will be activated at the crown."

At the end of the staircase they stepped upwards into the

crown. A golden halo of light filled the atmosphere, and a gentle midrange hum reverberated through the space and inside their heads.

"The vibration is now opening up your crown chakra. High vibrations of energy are entering your body through the crown chakra, and filling your aura. This is energy is also known as prana or chi."

Richard and Rose felt weightless, as if their physical bodies didn't exist, and the burdens they had carried for centuries, incarnation after incarnation, were being lifted. They were held in the absolute joy of pure unconditional love.

Rose instinctively took the pinecone shaped relic from her chest and held it, running her finger over the rounded edges, and along the ridged surface. She acknowledged the thousands of years it had waited, and all the people it took to guard it, including her own great-grandfather. Now here she was, at the top of the Statue of Liberty, knowing it had to be left behind at the monument, but where?

Richard wrapped his hand around hers, and an invisible force guided their two hands, pushing them gently under the rim of the crown, behind the iron framework. "Slowly, and accurately, their hands were moved, until the piece slid into a space, where it fit like a jigsaw puzzle piece.

"America went from being nothing to the greatest super power in a short space of time. This is because the crown chakra is located here, in New York City," Gela continued.

Gela touched both of their third eyes at the same time, lifting them from the planes of the human mind, to the plateaus of divinity. Projected in front of them, as if on an etheric movie screen, were scenes that could only be described as the rise, fall and return of America. The information put forth was narrated by Gela.

The vision began with Moses holding the Ten Commandments, blessing the twelve tribes of Israel. Richard witnessed himself as Aholiab, and Bartholdi as Bezaleel, crafting the Ark of the Covenant.

"Moses passed on the knowledge of esoteric Stonemasonry; how to encode matter with spiritual energy. This alchemy was carried over centuries. It was passed on through initiation and ritual, to men and women who had proven themselves honourable and worthy. At times, it was driven underground in order to stop those that sought to use the power for their own selfish ends. Thus, the mystery schools were born. This knowledge of encoding was, and has always been, used in sacred geometry in both ancient and modern buildings, hidden in plain sight, culminating in this place where we are standing. Those with this knowledge became the Masonic Brotherhood."

Pictures flashed before them: Liberty's codes, the eleven pointed star fort base, the pyramid-like pedestal, the double helix staircase, and the seven rays on her crown, ushering people along a journey of ascension – if and when a soul was ready to be in service to the principle of oneness.

Then, as if changing a channel with a remote control, the vision faded and was replaced by a scene of the original nine men guarding the entrance to the Temple of Solomon, which housed the Ark. The entrance, or 'Solomon's Gate' was a door with the picture of John the Baptist that hung on the wall in Templecombe.

"The original Knights Templar," Gela said. "The Knights established the foundation for modern banking with the highest of principles. They took vows of poverty. They created the first safety deposit boxes, and cheque systems, so pilgrims to the holy land wouldn't be vulnerable to thieves. They used their money for good, not for personal use," Gela explained.

"So the Knights were the guardians of knowledge and relics, and the forerunners of modern banking, while the Masons were the encoders," Rose said, half out loud.

Next came visions of George Washington, the founding fathers, and the signing of the Declaration of Independence in 1776.

"These men, many of them Masons, created the physical foundation of freedom in America. The Declaration and the Constitution are writs from on high, oaths to the Creator established in America since the beginning. The Declaration was the birthday of 'freedom'. Freedom from religious and political oppression. Though noble and altruistic, they didn't yet possess the consciousness to live up to its principles in the highest. They took others' freedom through slavery, and genocide. Remember, Moses led his people away from slavery. The Masons were initiates of Moses, so America has to live up to the highest of ideals. Then another righteous soul incarnated, with higher understanding, and devoted his life to freedom for everyone."

In 1863, Abraham Lincoln delivered the Gettysburg Address. "This nation, under God, shall have a new birth of freedom – and that government of the people, by the people, for the people, shall not perish from the earth." Forces were set in motion to stop this freedom from coming into being, by those who wanted to remain in the old power-over paradigm, but the movement had already begun," Gela continued.

"The ending of slavery was the next physical manifestation of the future spiritual freedom that America is being prepared for, and will take responsibility for spreading outwards. Freedom, my dear children, has many levels. There is religious and political freedom, physical freedom – as in the slaves – and economic freedom. This all culminates in spiritual freedom. Lincoln represents the archetype of individual integrity and equality. Just over a year later, in 1865, the same year as Lincoln's assassination and the end of the Civil War in the Unites States, Laboulaye received inspiration. At the dinner party he proposed a gift to America, a monument to liberty."

Then came scenes of the different waves of immigration: the Native Americans, followed by the first colonists, then the English, Northern Europeans and indentured servants, followed by the Chinese, Eastern Europeans and Russians.

"America holds the energy of people from all over the world, and represents every man. It is not by chance that the United Nations headquarters is here," Gela said.

Next came scenes of boom time, New York in the roaring twenties, a time when the United States gained dominance in world finance.

"There was a big change in lifestyle and culture. Media was filled with celebrities, women got the right to vote, there was massive industrial growth, automobiles, telephones, and a consumer driven culture was born."

The time of Maison's heyday, Rose thought.

Scenes from the Wall Street Crash of 1929 and the start of the Great Depression were particularly hard to watch. Businessmen, having lost their positions, jumped out of windows, believing they'd lost their power.

"The crash had to happen. Businesses had become greedy, representing only those in power. America had lost her way," Gela explained.

The picture changed again to the horrifying images of the annihilation of Twin Towers, whose demise engulfed lower Manhattan in an inferno of ash and smoke.

"Symbolically, the Twin Towers were Solomon's Gate, leading to personal liberty," Gela said, while a picture of the Twin Towers, with Liberty in between them appeared. The World Trade Center, the banking capital, whose principles were originally founded by the Knights Templar, were meant to serve humanity, not rob it. However, those that occupied high positions couldn't integrate the energy, and so manifested its opposite: greed, selfishness, power-over, corruption, excess. The Twin Towers, which still exist on the etheric plain, are a design incorporating sacred geometry representing duality, opposites: male/female, sun/moon, light/dark, good/evil and yin/yang. You will see this same design on the front of every cathedral throughout Europe – two towers at the front."

Richard and Rose listened, transfixed.

"The final days of opposites are coming to an end. Union is coming."

Finally, one tower appeared where the Twin Towers once stood.

"The Freedom Tower's spire reaches a total height of one thousand, seven hundred and seventy-six feet, which is an intentional reference to the year when the Declaration of Independence was signed," Gela said. "Union. The rebirth. America is now ready. America herself, through her over-soul, the divine feminine principle, has gone through the process of ascension."

The images stopped, and standing before Richard and Rose was the most beautiful, luminescent being either had ever seen. It was Gela of the Lenape. Gela, the keeper of happiness. Gela, the principle of the Divine Mother incarnate, with her big brown almond-shaped eyes, in her Native American dress, moccasins, and Wampum belt.

"We were a matriarchal and peace-loving tribe who cared and looked after each other. The feminine was honoured. We knew nothing of the concept of ownership. When the original settlers came, we helped them survive, showed them how to use the land, taught them how to grow corn, and other staple foods. Then the settlers began the separation from the mother, and slowly the patriarchs dominated. They sought power for themselves." Gela lowered her head as she continued. "We revered our mother and appreciated her bounty. As a people, we had a natural and established connection with the spirit world. We honoured it, and spirit took care of us. The settlers tried to break our connection, and broke our spirit. We knew we were living on a holy spot, a spot established from the beginning, as the place where the divine feminine would be personified, and held. There were Master Masons among them who preserved the ancient and sacred rites, protecting them for centuries until the time was right, but, as I showed you, the first settlers didn't have the consciousness fully, which is why our dear brother George Washington crossed the tides of time and space to give back the Wampum belt, in order to make amends and restore balance. One of America's karmic lessons is the right use of money and power. America lost its way, almost destroyed itself, but is now making the return journey. It will make further amends with the native people. The everyman put the pennies in to give Liberty her physical form. America has to set an example for the world. This is her last karmic responsibility. It must bring back the lost connection, preserve and honour the earth, not pillage it."

Gela turned their two bodies towards each other, and like a spider, spun a web of light into a three dimensional flower of life, the template from which all life springs. She then placed them inside it and weaved an outer case, like a cocoon from their feet to the top of their heads. It was dark inside, and Rose and Richard fell into a deep dreamy sleep, like a set of conjoined twins, the exact balance of male and female, sharing one higher mind, ready to be reborn. Gela's voice was faint as they re-entered three dimensional reality, and the denseness of their bodies returned.

"Maison is ready for its next phase, Maison..." The name echoed, as Gela's voice started to fade. "Freedom for one, freedom for all. The Divine Feminine has been restored, and the balance on earth will return."

The entire experience lasted only a few minutes, but it felt as if hours had passed.

Words were unnecessary, and Rose and Richard were silent as they descended the statue. They spoke very little all the way back to Rose's apartment. She thought of her father, and then wondered why the word 'Maison' came so strongly in the vision at the monument. She hoped everything was okay with her Mom and Dad. She couldn't wait to see them, and tell them everything.

CHAPTER 20

ROSE COHEN
New York City
Present Day

Samuel, Elizabeth, and Edith jumped out from the back corner booth when they saw Richard and Rose come through the door. It was a spectacle, considering all three were over seventy years old.

"My darling girl, you look like a different woman, so relaxed, so happy!" Elizabeth exclaimed, throwing her arms around her daughter, before turning to Richard, who stood somewhat shyly next to her. "Tell me all about it."

"Come. Sit down, you two. We want to hear everything!" Edith interrupted.

Samuel gave Rose a big hug. "I'm so glad my girl's back. It's only been a week, but I missed you so much."

Rose sensed that something wasn't quite right. Her perceptions were heightened, but even if they weren't she'd know by the look in her father's eyes. She couldn't put her finger on it, but she picked up on an undercurrent. Her father's heart was breaking, and she could feel it in her own. "Okay, but first, what's going on, Dad?"

Samuel saw a light in her eyes that he hadn't seen for years, and he didn't want to take it away. Rose was glowing.

"I've got something to tell you," her parents said, both at the exact same time.

"You first," they said at the same time again.

Richard laughed, and Rose relaxed back into her place.

"Oh, how I've missed you, honey," Samuel said, again.

"Honey, your father has something to tell you," Edith broke in. "It's really important, and it's not going to be easy to hear."

Rose felt as if someone had punched her in the solar plexus.

"You're not sick are you, Dad?"

"No, not physically, but I have to admit, my heart is a little sad."

"Why, Dad? Tell me."

"Well, I've been thinking for a long time," he looked towards Elizabeth. "*We've* been thinking. We're getting older. We're tired."

"I know, Dad."

"Well," he took a deep breath, and gathered his emotions. "We're ready to let Maison go now. We had an appraiser in while you were away. There's lots of interest in the building. We can make a *lot* of money. You'll be secure for the rest of your life," he sighed. "And your mom and I can finally have that peaceful life by the lake in Connecticut. We've even made some new friends there."

Rose grinned.

"Now, that was not the reaction I was expecting."

"Dad. You're not going to believe it. So much has happened to me," she took Richard's hand. "To us."

Noticing the ring on Rose's finger, Edith gently lifted her hand into her own. "Well, well, we do have some news, don't we?"

"Before we go into that, I need to say this. Edith, Dad, Mom, Richard and I had a long talk this morning. I could see that running this place was getting to be too much for you, and to be honest, the girl who left last week could not have stepped in to take on the responsibility," Rose said, lowering her head. "I think you've both known that for some time. But

I'm pleased to say that that girl has gone, and a new woman sits before you. Our journey together was full of synchronicities and magic. Most magical of all was our journey yesterday back to the Statue of Liberty. Remember? Ananda told us we needed to go there."

"Yes," Edith said.

"Dad, there is a divine hand at play. Maison is ready for its next phase. You're ready to let go, and we are ready to step in." Rose saw tears in her father's eyes. "Oh, don't be upset, Dad."

"These are tears of joy from every cell of my being. Happy tears. This place is my history, your history, America's history! Knowing that it'll stay in the family, and I can still come and help out, or just hang out, well, I can retire in peace now."

"When did you make the decision?" Rose asked her father.

"That night at Edith's with Ananda. I just knew it was time." He turned to Richard. "So, Richard. Are you gonna make my girl an honest woman?"

"Dad! Please!"

"Yes, Mr Cohen," he answered lifting Rose's hand to show them the ring. "You betcha!"

"Mazeltov!" Edith cried.

"Mazeltov!" they all joined in.

"Millie, bring a bottle of champagne, the best we got. Rose and Richard are getting married!" Samuel shouted, and gathered everyone around the table, just as *his* father had done all those years ago. "My girl's turned into a fine woman!" he shouted.

Rose put out her hand to show everyone her ring. "Congratulations, darling. But I want you to know that with or without that ring you've turned into a fine woman, my gorgeous daughter. It's you. You are, and have always been a kind and loving soul. Now you have realised this," he hugged her tightly. "That's all I've ever wanted for you. But this," he pointed at Richard, "is also great news and reason to celebrate!"

Millie, had retrieved a special bottle of Dom Perignon from the cellar. "Let me do the honours, Millie," Samuel said, taking the bottle. Like an expert, he unwrapped the foil, twisted the Muselet six half turns, and put his hand over the cork. It popped with such force that it flew out of his hand and hit the crystal chandelier, causing it to sway back and forth. The lights twinkled even more than usual. "I haven't done that in over twenty years!" Sam laughed.

"It's as if the shop itself is celebrating, giving its blessing," Elizabeth said, passing the glasses around. Even Richard had one.

"Excuse me. Sorry to interrupt," Millie said. There are some people at the door from the Salvation Army. They'd like to put a collection box out for the homeless.

Samuel always supported the Salvation Army. He liked the organisation's no-nonsense approach and grass roots action on the streets. "Send them over."

"Put it over there on the counter, next to the cash register," he instructed.

"Gracias, my friend."

Edith looked up. "Excuse me, son, where do I know you from?"

"Hey!" Richard exclaimed. "Look at you. What a coincidence. I just thought about you yesterday. Wondered how you were doing."

Miguel was clean shaven, and nicely dressed, but the biggest difference was the look of peace in his eyes, the hard edge was completely gone.

"Oh, my friends! *Dios mio!* I can't believe it! Where's the other man with the long hair? I've been praying to meet him again! He saved my life. Gave me another chance. I'm back with God, and committed to a life of service. Like he said, it was all meant to be."

"He's gone back to India, I'm afraid," Richard said.

"I must meet him again."

Edith interrupted. "You know what, Miguel, leave us your contact details – let us know where we can reach you. I will gladly take you there one day, and you can thank him in person."

"Thank you, Jesus. My prayers have been answered." Miguel left with the others, after writing down his details on a napkin, with an extra bounce in his step.

The five of them didn't move from the table until closing time that night. They talked. They laughed. They talked about the past, and they talked about the future. Richard and Rose told them everything that had happened while they were away, and during their visit to the Statue of Liberty.

"You'll have to excuse me a moment," Elizabeth said, and left the table.

"I hope I haven't said anything to upset her." Rose set down her champagne glass, but within a moment her mother had returned, and handed Rose a walking stick.

"I've kept this for a long time, Rose, and when you mentioned the pinecone shaped relic, I knew it had to be yours."

Rose took the stick, and admired its design. *It's made of Acacia.* The stick itself had a spiral pattern, and the handle was shaped like a pinecone, of all things.

"It was your great-grandfather's."

Rose remembered him holding the stick in the photograph on the wall upstairs... of him at Templecombe. She was utterly speechless and surprised by the incredibly powerful energy emanating from it. A vibration similar to the holy relic. She held the pinecone and frowned, it felt slightly loose. She twisted it, and found that it unscrewed. The stick was hollow. She turned it upside down, and a parchment fell out. Everyone gasped. Carefully uncurling the paper, she held it up to the light from a candle on the table. "'By the sword, through the heart, to the crown. Freedom and Liberty for all. Thy kingdom come. Thy Will be done. On earth as it is in heaven. Lux In Coronam.'"

"It's as if he's travelled through time," Rose said to Richard.

"Please someone, Google translate *Lux In Coronam.*"

Edith already had her phone on the table, and quickly typed in the words.

"The Light in the Crown."

Rose thought back to the picture of her great-grandfather with the cane and the bible, and Christ's crown of thorns, and Liberty's crown of light. *The balance of the masculine and feminine.*

At the end of a very long day that had slipped well into the evening, and after several bottles of bubbly, Samuel summoned the courage to ask, "My darlings. What is your vision for the future of our dear Maison?"

"If you don't mind my saying so, sir, any changes that happen here will have to be with your blessing. We wouldn't have it any other way."

Rose interrupted. "Richard and I plan to live together in my apartment, and we'll keep the downstairs as is – a people place, a heart place. It always has been, and must continue to be, but we have a vision for the upper apartment and upper room, Grandma and Grandpa's old place."

Samuel nodded in approval, recalling the days when he took over from his father, Morris, knowing that changes were needed in order bring in the next phase.

"You have my blessing to make any changes. I trust you, darling. And you, Richard."

"I'm so relieved that this place is continuing. My heart is full of joy. I know that it will inspire many in the future, and I look forward to the new," said Edith.

CHAPTER 21

Settled inside the small wooden hut, Ananda removed his prayer shawl from the tattered sack, wrapped it around his shoulders, and knelt before a very old, but sturdy acacia wood altar. He recited an ancient Sanskrit prayer as he lit a candle and incense stick, then twisted himself into a cross-legged position. He chanted the *Gayathiri Mantra* with focused attention on his third eye, breathing deeply and rhythmically, until he entered a transcendent state, a timeless space beyond self, of total inner peace.

"The Golden Age has begun," said the voice of Ananda's inner guide. "But always remember, the *journey there* is the sacred prayer."

EPILOGUE

LIBERTY CALLS
Always and Forever

"I am Gela. I am 'Libertas'. I am a beacon, a lighthouse. I am a living Goddess of Freedom embodied in a physical statue. I am calling all my children, at all stages of evolution, to come home to me, and to spiritual freedom. Receive my blessing. As you ascend through my body, your new consciousness develops. At my crown, you will be reborn. I am love. I am compassion. I am empathy. I am forgiveness, and understanding. I will heal your wounded parts with unconditional love. I will, as I always have, work with you at whatever degree of receptivity you come with. You will take the new consciousness back to your towns, cities, and countries, and will work with the higher good for all. Peace and harmony will be established within and without, and the promise of heaven on earth will be fulfilled. With my blessing, with my grace."
    Liberty
    Divine Mother

About the Authors

We are an Irish and American, Gemini and Sagittarius couple who live in Glastonbury, Somerset. Our book draws on over two decades of running Divine Light Tours, specialising in transformational journeys to the ancient and mystical sites of the UK, Ireland, and Scotland. We have two self-catering properties in Glastonbury for pilgrims and tourists alike.

John is psychic, a healer, and a practitioner of the Infinite Way. Over twenty years ago, John was 'told' in meditation that there was a sacred site in America that would be revealed when the time was right. When we started co-writing, the site was revealed, and became the premise for this book.

Meredith has a BA with a focus in Creative Writing, is a qualified alternative therapist and perfumer, and most important to her, a mother and friend.

Websites:
divinelightcentre.co.uk
divinelighttours.com

Research Index:

Chapter 3
www.masonicworld.com/education/articles/Masonry-and-the-statue-of-liberty.htm

Chapter 6
www.foundationsmag.com/civility.html
George Washington's Rules of Civility and Decent Behaviour ...In company and conversation

Chapter 15
www.nps.gov/stli/learn/historyculture/joseph-pulitzer.htm

As an article published in *New York World* on March 16, 1885 argued,

We must raise the money! The World is the people's paper, and now it appeals to the people to come forward and raise the money. The $250,000 that the making of the Statue cost was paid in by the masses of the French people- by the working men, the tradesmen, the shop girls, the artisans- by all, irrespective of class or condition. Let us respond in like manner. Let us not wait for the millionaires to give us this money. It is not a gift from the millionaires of France to the millionaires of America, but a gift of the whole people of France to the whole people of America.

The article's appeal was so popular that by August 11, 1885, the World collected over $100,000 in donations - most donations being about $1 or less. Roughly 125,000 people contributed to the completion of the pedestal thanks to Pulitzer's crusade. In thanks, the World published the names of each person who made a contribution (no matter its size), an act that also advanced the sales of Pulitzer's newspaper. Pulitzer died on October 29, 1911.

Chapter 18
www.masonicworld.com/education/articles/Masonry-and-the-statue-of-liberty.htm

www.masonicworld.com/education/articles/Masonry-and-the-statue-of-liberty.htm

Made in the USA
Middletown, DE
24 November 2020